Anna turned so she could get a look at this vision of masculinity, and froze when she saw the man who was walking towards her.

He was certainly tall and blond, and handsome too, so she could understand why the receptionist was so smitten with him. She'd felt exactly the same the first time she'd seen him, too. He'd had more than just good-looks going for him. He'd been intelligent, funny, kind—all the qualities she'd admired in a man.

That first meeting had quickly been followed by a second and a third. By the fourth she'd known that she had found the man she'd wanted to spend her life with.

'Hello, Anna. Good to see you again. How are you?'

His voice was soft and low, and she felt a shiver pass through her. In the past three years she had done her best to forget him. Every time his face had sprung to mind she had blanked it out. She had tried to erase him from her life, but she hadn't succeeded in erasing him from her heart.

Dear Reader

I always get a thrill when I start to write another book in my on-going Dalverston General Hospital* series. Although the hospital and the people who work there are purely figments of my imagination, they have become very real to me over the past few years. I feel as though I am setting off to visit some dear friends when I start off on the first page!

In THEIR LITTLE CHRISTMAS MIRACLE, Sam Kearney finds himself thrust into a situation he never expected. He is stunned when he takes up a new post at Dalverston General Hospital and discovers that Anna is working there. He has never got over losing her, although it soon becomes clear that Anna has done everything possible to forget about him.

Anna is shocked when she realises that her feelings for Sam are as strong as they ever were. She has done her best to put their marriage behind her, sure in her own mind that she was right to insist on a divorce. She can never give Sam the family he yearns for. It will take a miracle to make them both change their minds, but it's Christmas time in Dalverston, and sometimes miracles do happen....

I hope you enjoy this book as much as I enjoyed telling Sam and Anna's story. Have a wonderful Christmas, wherever you are.

Love

Jennifer

*For a full list of all the books in the Dalverston General series, please visit my website at www.jennifer-taylor.com

THEIR LITTLE CHRISTMAS MIRACLE

BY
JENNIFER TAYLOR

MILLS & BOON®

Pure reading pleasure

First published in Great Britain 2007
Harlequin Mills & Boon Limited,
Eton House, 18-24 Paradise Road, Richmond, Surrey TW9 1SR

ISBN: 978 0 263 19714 3

Set in Times Roman 10½ on 12¾ pt
15-1007-46471

Printed and bound in Great Britain
by Antony Rowe Ltd, Chippenham, Wiltshire

THEIR LITTLE CHRISTMAS MIRACLE

Jennifer Taylor lives in the north-west of England with her husband Bill. She had been writing Mills & Boon® romances for some years, but when she discovered Medical™ Romances, she was so captivated by these heart-warming stories that she set out to write them herself! When she's not writing, or doing research for her latest book, Jennifer's hobbies include reading, travel, walking her dog and retail therapy (shopping!). Jennifer claims all that bending and stretching to reach the shelves is the best exercise possible. She's always delighted to hear from readers, so do visit her at www.jennifer-taylor.com

Recent titles by the same author:

DR FERRERO'S BABY SECRET*
DR CONSTANTINE'S BRIDE*
THE WOMAN HE'S BEEN WAITING FOR
A NIGHT TO REMEMBER

Mediterranean Doctors

CHAPTER ONE

HE RECOGNISED her voice as soon as he heard it on the car radio. It made no difference that it had been three years since they'd spoken because he remembered every nuance of those tones. The sound of her voice had been stored away along with all the other memories of their life together, both good and bad.

Sam Kearney's hand was shaking as he turned up the volume. He had tuned into the local radio station after he'd left the motorway. He hated being late on his first day in a new job and he'd been hoping to catch the hourly traffic bulletin, but instead he'd heard Anna, her voice sounding so sweetly familiar as it flowed into the car that it made him ache with longing. Three years may have passed but he still hadn't got over the pain of losing her.

'So what would be your advice to this young couple, Dr Carter?' the interviewer was saying now, and Sam grimaced.

He hadn't realised that Anna had reverted to her maiden name after their divorce and it hurt to know that she had wanted to erase him so completely from her life. They had been together for five years and despite how their marriage had ended, they had loved each other in the beginning.

'That they should try to take a more relaxed approach. Getting pregnant isn't a competition. It takes some couples a little longer than others, especially if the woman has been taking the Pill for a fairly lengthy period, as in this case. If nothing has happened after six months then I would suggest they see their GP and ask to be referred to a fertility specialist. However, I doubt if it will be necessary.'

'That sounds like excellent advice to me. Right, folks, that just about rounds off today's programme. We've been talking to Dr Anna Carter, a consultant in obstetric and gynaecological care at Dalverston General Hospital…'

Sam switched off the radio. He didn't need to hear any more. What he had heard already promised to create enough problems. He'd had no idea that Anna was working at Dalverston General. The last he'd heard she was still in London but obviously she'd decided to relocate. Now he needed to decide what he was going to do.

He had accepted the job as locum specialist registrar in Dalverston General's emergency department in good faith, but would it be right to take it up now that he knew Anna was working there? How would she feel about him coming back into her life, even if it was only on a temporary basis?

His contract was for three months and he wouldn't stay on after that. Three months was the maximum amount of time he worked anywhere, even though the agency was always asking him to extend his contracts. However, he'd discovered that three months was ideal—long enough to be useful but not so long that he was tempted to put down roots. He would have been happy to spend three months at Dalverston, too, but could he face the thought of raking up the past?

Sam's mouth compressed as he glanced at the dashboard clock. There was just an hour left before he was due at the hospital to start his first shift. He would have to make up his mind soon.

'Heard the show today, Anna—you were great. I didn't know we had our very own media star working here.'

'Tell me that again in the morning, will you?' Anna rolled her eyes. 'I don't feel much like a star at the moment. I'm shattered!'

'It has been a busy evening,' the ward sister agreed. She glanced at the empty bed by the door and sighed. 'It's such a shame about Marie. She was so desperate to have that baby.'

'It's very sad,' Anna concurred, struggling to keep a check on her emotions.

She hated it when one of her mums miscarried and it was even worse in this case. Marie Jones and her husband, Jack, had undergone several years of gruelling fertility treatment and they'd been overjoyed when Marie had discovered she was pregnant. Anna knew from her own experiences how stressful it was to go through the process of trying to conceive and she understood how devastated Marie must feel.

'Marie should be back from Theatre soon,' she said quickly, because it wouldn't help to dwell on her own situation. She had come to terms with the fact that she would never have a family of her own and now focused all her energies on helping other women fulfil their dreams of motherhood. It helped to take the edge off the pain, although it never fully went away. The only consolation was that at least Sam no longer had to suffer the heartache of being childless, too.

'I think we'll move her into a side room, if you don't mind, Wendy,' she said briskly, quelling that thought as well. 'I know the other women will be very sympathetic, but Marie probably won't feel like talking to anyone. If we put her in a side room, at least she and Jack can have some time to themselves.'

'I don't mind at all. I'll get the bed ready for when she comes back.' Wendy headed towards the corridor then paused when the office phone rang.

'It's OK, I'll get it,' Anna offered. 'It's probably Theatre to say that Marie is on her way down.'

'I hope so.' Wendy pulled a face. 'We've had two emergencies already and it isn't even midnight yet. I could do without another one.'

'Me too.'

Anna hurried into the office. Snatching the receiver off its rest, she tucked it into the hollow of her shoulder while she helped herself to a chocolate from a box one of their mums had given them as a leaving present. All her favourites had gone so it was either a coffee cream or a toffee. She chose the toffee and popped it in her mouth.

'Obs and gynae,' she announced, somewhat hampered by the sweet. 'Can I help you?

'It's ED,' a male voice announced. 'We have a young woman here who was involved in an RTA. She's one of your patients, apparently—Sarah Harris—and she says that she's thirty weeks pregnant with twins. She's experiencing some stomach cramps so can someone come down and take a look at her?'

'Uh-huh,' Anna mumbled, shifting the wedge of toffee to her other cheek.

'I take it that was a yes, so I'll expect you shortly.'

The line went dead before she could ask to whom she was speaking. Not that it really mattered, but the management had implemented a new system regarding internal phone calls. Every call had to be logged in the departmental diary. Nobody had explained why they were doing so, although Anna had heard on the grapevine that it was in case the hospital was ever sued for negligence. If the management could prove that the correct steps had been followed, it would minimise any damages they had to pay. The fact that they could also lay the blame for any mishap on an individual member of staff was a bonus, of course.

Anna scrawled 'ED' in the diary, added the time and initialled it then left. Wendy was just leaving the side room and she stopped to tell her where she was going.

'ED phoned. They've got Sarah Harris down there. RTA. She has stomach cramps, apparently.'

'Do you want me to alert Theatre?' Wendy offered immediately.

'Please. You'd better get onto Neonatal Intensive

Care, too. It's twins so that's going to make it doubly difficult.'

Wendy didn't say anything, but Anna could tell that she was worried, too. She mentally crossed her fingers as she stepped into the lift, hoping there would be enough incubators available if she had to deliver the babies. The last time she'd checked, NICU had been bursting at the seams and she hated to think that one of the babies might have to be ferried to another hospital.

ED was bustling when she arrived. There was just a week left until Christmas and the waiting room was packed with people who had been out celebrating. Anna skirted around a couple of drunks who were entertaining everyone with a noisy rendition of 'Silent Night' and headed for the desk, thanking her stars that she didn't work there. At least her mums were usually sober when she saw them!

'Hi. Someone phoned Obs and Gynae to say you have one of our patients down here.'

'Oh, that would be our new locum.' Polly, the receptionist, winked at her. 'You're in for a treat, Anna. He only started today and he's a real babe. Tall, blond, handsome—I tell you, I thought I'd died and gone to heaven when I saw him!'

Anna chuckled. 'He certainly seems to have made a big impression on you.'

'You're not kidding. Shame I'm married, really.' Polly glanced over Anna's shoulder and sighed. 'Here he comes now. Brace yourself.'

Anna turned so she could get a look at this vision of masculinity and froze when she saw the man who was walking towards her. He was certainly tall and blond, and handsome, too, so she could understand why the receptionist was so smitten with him. She'd felt exactly the same the first time she'd seen Sam, too. She'd always been wary of men who were too handsome but he'd had more than just good looks going for him. He'd been intelligent, funny, kind—all the qualities she'd admired in a man.

That first meeting had quickly been followed by a second and a third. By the fourth, she'd known that she had found the man she'd wanted to spend her life with. That he had felt the same about her had proved that they'd been meant for each other. They had married three months to the day after they'd met and they'd been happy too, so happy that she'd thought nothing could spoil their union, but she'd been wrong. In the end their love just hadn't been enough to sustain them.

'Hello, Anna. Good to see you again. How are you?'

His voice was soft and low, and she felt a shiver pass through her. She couldn't believe that she hadn't recognised his voice on the phone, although maybe it wasn't so surprising. In the past three years she had done her best to forget him. Every time his face had sprung to mind she had blanked it out, each time she had found herself thinking about him she had made herself stop. She had tried to erase him from her life but she hadn't succeeded in erasing him from her heart.

'Hello, Sam. This is a surprise. When did you start working here?' she asked as calmly as she could.

'Today.' He glanced past her and smiled at the receptionist who was eagerly following the conversation.

'Dr Carter and I are old friends. Isn't that a coincidence?'

'I...um, yes, it is,' Polly replied, sounding flustered as she suddenly remembered what she'd said to Anna.

Anna moved away from the desk, not wanting the receptionist to see how flustered *she* felt. It had never crossed her mind that Sam would turn up in Dalverston. The last she'd heard, he'd been in Australia, working for the Flying Doctor service. That had been a couple of years ago and she'd heard nothing since. It was hard to maintain an aura of calm as she followed him across the waiting room but she refused to let him see how rattled she felt. As Sam had put it so succinctly, they were old friends now—nothing more.

The thought stung a little and she cleared her throat. 'How is Sarah? Was she badly injured in the accident?'

'A few cuts and bruises—nothing serious, though.' Sam pushed open the door to Resus then stepped aside so she could precede him.

'Thank you.' Anna walked into the room, trying to ignore the tremor that rippled through her when her hand brushed his arm as she passed him. Typically, Sam had spurned the use of a white coat and was wearing a plain blue shirt with the sleeves rolled up to his elbows. In the bright lights of Resus the thick blonde hair on his forearms gleamed like strands of gold and she shivered again as she recalled the softness of the down brushing against her fingertips. It took a massive effort to force herself to concentrate as they made their way to the bed.

'Hello, Sarah. I hear you've been in the wars tonight,' she said, smiling at the young woman.

'It was awful, Dr Carter. Mike and I were just driving along when this van came out of nowhere and hit us— Oh-h-h!'

Sarah broke off and groaned. Anna frowned when she saw the girl clutch her stomach. 'Is there any staining?' she asked, turning to Sam.

'No. There's no blood coming from the vagina and her waters haven't broken. The cervix isn't dilated either.' He glanced at Sarah. 'The cramps seem to be getting worse, don't they, Sarah?'

'They do,' she gasped. She turned imploring eyes on Anna. 'I'm not in labour, am I, Dr Carter? It's far too soon for that.'

'I'm going to examine you and then I'll have a clearer idea what's going on,' Anna explained gently.

She carefully palpated Sarah's abdomen, feeling concerned when she discovered how rigid it felt. Placing her hand flat on the young woman's swollen tummy, she waited for a moment and felt the unmistakable signs of another contraction beginning.

'We need to get her up to the maternity unit immediately,' she told Sam, *sotto voce,* while Sarah rode out the pain.

'The babies are on their way?' he said just as softly.

'Yes. We might be able to stop the contractions but I'm not holding out much hope. I think things are too far advanced for that.'

'What are the babies' chances?'

Anna felt a lump come to her throat when she saw the concern in his eyes. Sam's ability to empathise with his patients was one of his greatest gifts as a doctor. He could never treat a patient as just another case—he cared too much. However, it was even more poignant in a situation like this. He understood how devastated Sarah would be if her babies didn't survive because he had been through the heartache of longing for a child. It made Anna see that no matter how calm he appeared on the surface, the scars ran deep.

'Quite good. Thirty weeks is early, but babies born well before that time can and do survive,' she said with a detachment she didn't feel. 'Plus, I know from the most recent scan that both twins are a good size and that will go in their favour.'

'That's good to hear.'

He didn't try to hide the fact that he was concerned, as a lot of men might have done, and Anna turned away. Although Sam might be happy to let her see that he was emotionally vulnerable, she certainly wasn't. She asked one of the nurses to phone for a porter then explained to Sarah that she was going to transfer her to the maternity unit.

The young mum was obviously scared by what was happening but Anna reassured her as best she could. She wished she could promise Sarah that the twins would be all right but it was still very much at the if, and, but stage. *If* everything went smoothly *and* there were no major complications, the babies had a good chance of surviving. *But* it was impossible to foresee every problem that might occur.

The porter arrived a few minutes later and they wheeled Sarah out of Resus. Sam accompanied them to the lift, holding Sarah's hand as they went down the corridor. The poor girl clutched tight hold of him as the lift doors opened.

'You'll tell Mike where I am, won't you? I don't want to be on my own…'

'And you won't be.' Sam smiled at her. 'As soon as Mike's arm has been set, I shall personally escort him to Maternity. That's a promise!'

'Thank you.' Sarah managed a smile then they were in the lift and the doors were closing.

Anna's last impression before they shut were of Sam's face and she knew that the picture of him, standing there, would stay with her throughout the night. Sam was trusting her to take care of Sarah and her babies, and she wouldn't let him down. It was something she could do for him that might help to ease the pain. Maybe she hadn't been able to give him the child he had longed for, but she could try and make sure these babies survived.

CHAPTER TWO

MORNING crept in with very little fanfare. It was one of those bleak December days that Sam always loathed. He collected his bag from the staffroom and headed for the stairs. Although he was bone weary after the busy night he'd had, he wanted to make a last check on Sarah Harris and her twins.

A smile softened the tired lines around his mouth as he made his way up to the maternity unit, two floors above. Both babies had survived and were currently in the neonatal intensive care unit. Anna had phoned to tell him the good news a couple of hours before and he wanted to thank her for that as well. At least they were on speaking terms and that was something to be grateful for.

He sighed as he rang the bell to gain admittance to the maternity unit. Three years on and he was still grateful for any crumbs. He had tried to put their marriage behind him but he hadn't succeeded. The pain was as raw today as it had been when it had happened. He had even tried getting back onto the dating merry-go-round in the hope that it would help if he met someone else, but it had been a disaster. He simply wasn't interested in other women—Anna had spoiled him for anyone else. It seemed that he was destined to live out his days alone and the thought certainly didn't add a sparkle to an already grey day. Having grown up in a noisy and rambunctious family, he couldn't picture himself living like a hermit.

'Yes? Can I help you?'

Sam started when the door opened. He fixed a winsome smile to his mouth in the hope that it would gain him admittance to the unit. Security was tight in any maternity unit, and Dalverston's unit was no exception.

'I'm Sam Kearney, the new specialist reg from ED. I took care of Sarah Harris when she was brought in following her accident and I was wondering if it would be possible to sneak a look at her babies.'

'I'm sorry, Dr Kearney, but only relatives are admitted to the unit,' the nurse said firmly. She started to close the door and Sam hurriedly stuck his foot into the gap.

'Are you sure you can't make an exception in this instance?' he beseeched her. 'It's been one heck of a night in ED and a glimpse of those little ones would do wonders to make up for it.'

'I'm sorry but it really isn't possible.'

The nurse stared pointedly at his foot. Sam sighed as he withdrew it. 'OK. Thanks anyway,' he said as he turned to leave.

'Sam?'

He spun round when he heard Anna's voice and felt his heart carry on spinning when he saw her walking towards him. Her dark brown hair had come lose from its customary elegant knot, soft little wisps curling around her small ears. There were shadows under her brown eyes, which told their own tale about the night she'd had too, but she still looked incredibly beautiful. It was an effort not to drool as she stopped in front of him.

'What are you doing here?' she demanded in a crisp tone, which immediately brought him back to earth. Anna certainly wouldn't appreciate him having lustful thoughts about her at this stage.

'I was hoping to get a look at the twins.' He glanced at the nurse who was standing guard by the door in case he tried any more salesman-type tactics, and shrugged. 'However, it appears that only relatives are allowed into the unit.'

'That's right.' Anna glanced at the nurse as well and there was a hint of uncertainty on her face, which intrigued him. Was she actually considering bending the rules for his benefit?

The thought gave him a definite boost in the ego department and he smiled at her. 'A glimpse of those little ones would be the perfect antidote to all the other sights I've seen tonight.'

'I can imagine.' Anna wavered a moment longer but Sam didn't say anything else. It was up to her to decide if he was trustworthy or not.

'I can't see any harm in letting you have a quick look at them,' she said suddenly. She turned to the nurse. 'I'll sign Dr Kearney in, Maureen, and escort him to NICU.'

'Of course, Dr Carter.'

Maureen didn't look pleased as she relinquished her door duties and Sam couldn't help feeling a little guilty. 'I didn't mean to cause any problems by wheedling my way in here,' he explained as Anna led him to the desk and wrote his name in the visitors' book.

'You haven't.' She didn't look at him as she initialled the entry. 'If I hadn't wanted to admit you, I wouldn't have done so. Now, if you'd care to leave your bag here and follow me, I'll take you through.'

She was all business as she headed along the corridor. Sam sighed as he dumped his holdall behind the desk and followed her. Anna was making it clear that nothing *he* did could influence her in any way. It had been the same three years ago when she had told him that she thought they should get divorced. He had tried to convince her that he could live with the thought of them never having children, but she had refused to listen to him. Once Anna made up her mind, there was no turning her, and it seemed she hadn't changed in that respect.

It was a sobering thought, although Sam wasn't sure why it bothered him so much. He did his best to put it out of his mind as they stopped outside NICU. Anna sprayed her hands with alcohol rub and waited while he followed suit, then she keyed in the security code and opened the door. There was a stack of disposable gowns on a trolley just inside the room and Sam nodded when she told him that he would have to wear one.

He slipped his arms into the garment and fastened the sticky tags at the shoulder and the waist then accompanied her across the room, his heart aching as he looked at the tiny scraps of humanity they passed. Only the very sickest babies were brought to this unit and he knew that some of them wouldn't survive. It was painful to imagine what these children's parents must be going through.

'Here they are.'

Anna stopped beside two incubators and Sam felt a lump come to his throat when he saw the babies for the first time. They were so small that each was barely as big as the palm of one of his hands. They were lying on sheepskin rugs, and were completely naked apart from nappies and doll-sized crocheted bonnets to help maintain their body heat.

'They're so tiny!' he exclaimed in awe as he bent to take a closer look.

'Sam weighed in at three pounds and Anna was two pounds six ounces,' Anna explained quietly. 'Not a bad weight, considering.'

Sam's head shot up. 'Sam and Anna? You mean that Sarah has named them after us?'

'She and Mike insisted.' Anna fiddled with a tiny tube that was supplying oxygen to baby Sam. 'It was a nice a gesture, wasn't it?'

'It was a lovely thing to do,' Sam mumbled, the wretched lump in his throat growing bigger by the second.

He turned away, not wanting Anna to see how moved he felt. How many times had they discussed what they would call their children? He had insisted that if they'd had a girl, he'd wanted her to have Anna as her middle name, and Anna had said that she'd wanted their son to be called Sam after him. Now these two precious children bore their names and he couldn't begin to describe how he felt, and didn't want to try.

'Yes, it was.'

There was a tautness to Anna's voice that made him glance at her and his heart ached when he saw the tears that shimmered in her eyes for a moment before she blinked them away. She was all business as she called over one of the nursing staff and ran through the twins' obs.

Sam waited in silence while the two women discussed the twins' treatment. Apart from the fact that he didn't want to interrupt such an important discussion, he had nothing worthwhile to say. Telling Anna that he understood why she was upset would be the wrong thing to do. She had tried to erase him from her life and bringing up the past would be a mistake. He had to accept that as far as Anna was concerned they were just two people who happened to work together now.

It was painful to face that fact when he knew that he would never be able to think of her that way in a million years. His feelings for Anna were as strong as they'd ever been, but he had to learn how to disguise them if he was to build any kind of a relationship with her. Maybe it was foolish to consider the idea, but he simply couldn't bear to work in the same building and not be able to speak to her. So maybe he was accepting crumbs again, but if crumbs were all he could have, he would settle for them rather than nothing at all.

'I'll be in tonight to check on them.' Anna handed back the twins' notes and turned to him. 'Are you ready to leave?'

Sam nodded, not wanting to ruin things by over-staying his welcome. 'Yes, thanks. It was good to get a glimpse of them. I appreciate it.'

'No problem.'

She led him back across the room, pausing by the door while they deposited their gowns in the bin before heading out to the corridor. They reached the reception desk and Anna paused again while she signed him out.

Sam sighed as he glanced at his watch and discovered that it was barely seven a.m. There were still a couple of hours to go before he could turn up at his lodgings and he wasn't sure how to fill in the time. Maybe he should have some breakfast, although the thought of visiting the staff canteen wasn't the most appealing of prospects.

'Can you recommend anywhere to eat apart from the staff canteen?' he asked as Anna put her pen in her pocket. He shrugged when she looked at him in surprise. 'I'm not due at my lodgings until nine and I could do with something to eat before then.'

'Lodgings?'

'Uh-huh. The accommodation officer found me somewhere to stay. I've got the address here.' He dug a piece of paper out of his pocket. 'Apparently, my landlady is a Mrs Harvey of number 3 Brookside Cottages.'

'Your landlady?' Anna's brows rose in astonishment. 'Why on earth didn't you find yourself a flat?'

'Too much hassle. I'll only be here for a couple of months and it isn't worth getting settled into a flat only to have to move back out again.' He held up the canvas holdall, deeming it wiser not to mention that it contained all his worldly goods. 'This way, all I need is a change of clothes.'

'It's one way of looking at it, I suppose,' she said, her tone indicating that she thought he was crazy. She didn't actually come out and say so, though, and Sam grimaced. Obviously, Anna was determined not to be drawn into his life or his affairs.

'So where's the best place around here to have breakfast?' he prompted, returning the conversation to a relatively safe topic. He grinned at her. 'You always used to know the best places to eat so where do you recommend?'

'The transport café on the bypass.'

She gave him a rather strained smile and too late he realised that it hadn't been the most tactful thing to do, to remind her of the past like that. He hurried on. 'It's the real McCoy, is it? You can get a proper breakfast there?'

'Oh, yes.' Anna's smile relaxed a smidgen. 'Bacon, eggs, sausages, fried bread, beans…'

'Don't!' Sam held up his hand and groaned. 'My mouth is already watering.'

'Wait till you taste it,' she warned him with a wicked little chuckle. 'Al does the best fry-up in the world. Once you've tasted one of his breakfasts, you'll be spoiled for anyone else's.'

'I'll risk it.' Sam smiled back, feeling his heart overflow when he saw the laughter on her face. In the months leading up to their divorce there had been all too little to laugh about and it was wonderful to see her looking so relaxed. Maybe it was that thought which prompted him to say something he hadn't planned on saying.

'How about you, Anna? Are you willing to take the risk of being completely hooked and join me for one of Al's fabulous breakfasts?'

'And a large mug of tea, please.'

Anna moved away from the counter as Al finished writing their order on his pad. There was an empty table near the door so she headed in that direction, still not sure if it had been wise to join Sam for breakfast. She sighed as she pulled out one of the chairs and sat down. She could have refused if she'd wanted to, so why hadn't she? Because the thought of spending some time with Sam had been too tempting to resist?

'I hope the food's as good as you claim because I've ordered a double portion of everything.' Sam pulled out a chair and sat down, grinning broadly when she gasped. 'I may as well go the whole hog.'

'That's what you'll get,' she retorted. 'The whole hog. Al's portions aren't for the faint-hearted.'

'So I can see.'

Sam chuckled as he glanced around the café. Anna smiled as well as she followed his gaze. The place was crowded with truck drivers and an awful lot of them were on the heavy side. Long hours on the road combined with a calorie-laden diet had obviously taken their toll.

Her gaze moved back to Sam and she frowned when she realised that he'd lost weight since the last time she'd seen him. He'd always been leanly built but now his rangy six-foot frame looked even more sinewy. It made her wonder what he'd been doing in the intervening years and somehow that thought translated itself into a question.

'How come you took the job at Dalverston? The last I heard, you were in Australia.'

'That's right.' He leant back in his chair and sighed. 'I did almost a year with the Flying Doctor Service and I really enjoyed it, too. Australia's a great place to work. I was tempted to stay out there, in fact.'

'So what made you come back?' Anna asked curiously.

'Mum was diagnosed with breast cancer last year.' His expression sobered all of a sudden. 'It was a real shock, as you can imagine. As soon as I heard what had happened, I handed in my notice and came back to England.'

'I'm really sorry,' Anna said sincerely. She'd been very fond of Sam's parents—they had welcomed her into their family and had treated her like a daughter. Her own parents had moved to Florida after they'd retired and she saw them only infrequently so she had been particularly grateful for the kindness Mr and Mrs Kearney had shown her. Although she had broken off any contact with them after the divorce, she hated to think of Mary Kearney having to go through such a terrible ordeal.

'How is she now?' she asked quietly.

'Not too bad. She had a mastectomy and chemo, which wasn't much fun, but her consultant is very hopeful that they've caught it in time. She and Dad have gone over to Ireland to spend Christmas with the family.

Both my brothers live there now and my sister has decided that she'll go over as well. It will give Mum a real boost to spend some time with all her grandchildren.'

'Let's hope so,' Anna agreed softly. 'Give her my best wishes the next time you speak to her, will you?'

'Of course. She often asks about you and I know she'll be pleased to hear that you're all right.' He paused and looked deep into her eyes. 'You are, aren't you, Anna? All right, I mean—happy with your life?'

'Of course I am.' She gave a tinkly little laugh, which sounded false even to her ears, and hurried on. 'Why shouldn't I be?'

'No reason at all,' he said with a shrug.

Fortunately, Al arrived with their meal just then and the subject was dropped. However, as they tucked into the food, Anna could feel the question reverberating inside her head: was she happy with her life?

Maybe she could answer a resounding yes with regard to her work because the job in Dalverston had turned out to be everything she had hoped it would be. However, it would be a lie to claim that her personal life was everything she could wish for. Oh, she had her friends—more friends here than she'd had in London, in fact—but there was no escaping the fact that she often felt as though there was something missing from her life. Up till now she had told herself it was because she'd been unable to have the family she'd longed for, but was that the only reason?

Her eyes rested on Sam for a moment and she felt a searing pain run through her. Or was the real reason that without Sam in her life, she could never be truly happy?

CHAPTER THREE

'I AM completely *stuffed!*'

Sam leant back in his seat and groaned. He grimaced when Anna chuckled. 'OK, so you did warn me that Al's breakfasts were of historic proportions.'

'Shame you didn't listen, wasn't it?' she retorted, daintily mopping the last trace of egg yolk off her plate.

'I never thought you would resort to "I told you so" tactics,' Sam grumbled. 'A little sympathy wouldn't go amiss.'

'I'm all out of sympathy, I'm afraid.' She placed her knife and fork neatly on her plate and smiled at him. 'You did this to yourself, Sam Kearney, and now you will have to suffer the consequences.'

'I don't know when you became so hard-hearted,' he grouched, hamming it up for all he was worth. It had been ages since they'd indulged in this kind of light-hearted banter and he, for one, was enjoying it, probably more than he should be.

He closed his mind to that thought as he fixed a suitably woebegone expression to his face. 'Can't you rustle up even a smidgen of concern for the way I'm suffering?'

'Nope. Not even a smidgen. My advice to you is to grin and bear it.'

'That's not very kind, is it?' His hang-dog look obviously wasn't having the desired effect so he switched tactics. He summoned a smile, making sure Anna knew the effort it cost him. 'If the boot was on the other foot, I'd be positively *oozing* sympathy.'

'Like you did when we went picking strawberries that time?' she said sweetly. 'I don't recall you being very sympathetic when I broke out in a rash.'

'Maybe not, but it was your own fault, Anna.' He spread his hands wide open in gesture of bewilderment. 'You know very well that you break out in hives if you eat too many strawberries, yet you kept sneaking them out of the punnet whenever I wasn't watching.'

'So that's why you thought you were justified to laugh at my plight? You even had the cheek to call me Spotty Muldoon, as I recall!'

'Ah, but I did make up for it later,' he pointed out. 'I got through a whole bottle of calamine lotion that night, dabbing it on your spots to stop them itching.'

'I…um…don't remember.'

She looked away, making a great production out of drinking the last of her tea, but it didn't fool Sam for a second. She remembered as clearly as he did how he had treated her with the soothing lotion.

Heat flowed through him as the memories came flooding back and it was all he could do not to groan out loud in remembered ecstasy. What had started as a purely practical means to ease her discomfort had quickly turned into something far more erotic. Long before all the spots had been bathed, they had been swept away by passion. They had made love that night with an intensity that still had the power to stir him even now as he recalled it. He had never wanted any woman the way he had wanted Anna and he never would.

Sam pushed back his chair, unable to deal with thoughts like that when he was so tired. 'I don't know about you, but I'm just about out on my feet.'

'Me, too.'

Anna put her mug on the table and stood up. Sam could tell that she was as keen to leave as he was. Talking about the past was a strain for both of them and from this point on, he resolved, there must be no more harking back to the days when their lives had been intertwined.

'Thanks for agreeing to have breakfast with me,' he said politely as they left the café.

'Thank you for inviting me,' she said, equally formally.

They had come in separate cars and Sam paused when they reached the vehicles. 'It was my pleasure. Apart from the fact that it was good to have your company, Anna, there was another reason for the invitation,' he explained, knowing that he had to be truthful with her. 'I'm going to be working in Dalverston for the next three months and I don't want there to be any awkwardness if we bump into each other.'

'Me neither,' she agreed quietly. 'I'd like to think we could be friends, Sam.'

'That's what I want, too.' He took her hand and held it lightly in his, trying to ignore the leap his heart gave when his fingers closed around her far smaller ones.

Three years on and just the touch of her hand could make him feel giddy, he marvelled, even though he knew that he had to control such an excess of emotion. 'If we could have a chat, maybe share the odd cup of coffee, that would be great.'

'I can't see any reason why not.'

She withdrew her hand, her smile firmly fixed into place, yet he could tell how ambivalent she felt about him touching her. Maybe Anna wasn't as immune to him as he had thought.

His heart sang with joy at the idea before he ruthlessly battened it down again. 'Good. Now I'd better go and meet my new landlady. Fingers crossed that she doesn't turn out to be a real dragon.'

'Fingers *and* toes!' Anna replied with a laugh, but he heard the strain in her voice and felt his emotions see-saw once more.

He sighed as he got into his car because it would be foolish to hope for something that would never happen. They'd had their chance at happiness and they had failed. Their love hadn't been enough to bind them together, or enough to withstand the heartache of them not having the family they had yearned for. It would be stupid to think they could try again, stupid and danger-ous, too, because a heart once broken never really healed. He couldn't go through the pain of losing Anna all over again—it would destroy him. All he could hope for now was that they could be friends.

Anna drove straight home, trying not to think about what had happened in the last hour, but it was impossible. It had been enough of a shock to see Sam again, but what made it so much worse was that she felt so ambivalent towards him.

She'd never had any doubts about their divorce. She'd always known it had been the right thing to do. Her only concern had been to protect Sam from the heartache of being childless, and she would do exactly the same thing again today if it was necessary. However, she couldn't pretend that she didn't have any feelings for him.

She sighed as she drew up outside the tiny terraced cottage she had bought on the outskirts of the town. It had been built over a hundred years before to provide accommodation for one of the miners who had lived in the town. A whole family had once lived in this tiny two-up, two-down house—mother, father, umpteen children. It never failed to amaze her that so many people had crammed themselves into such a small space when it was barely big enough for her needs. However, it would have been silly to have bought a bigger house. There was just her, after all. No husband, no children, nothing and no one to clutter up the house or her life.

A wave of sadness filled her as she let herself in. Normally, she looked forward to returning home and considered the house as her sanctuary. She'd taken great care when decorating it, using neutral colours throughout—creams and taupe—with odd touches of gold and rust. The living room and kitchen were now one huge space and felt wonderfully light and airy. Steep stairs led to the first floor which now comprised one large bedroom and a luxurious bathroom.

Everything had been tailored to her needs, but as she tossed her coat onto the bed, Anna could derive very little pleasure from her surroundings. The house looked exactly like what it was: the home of a single woman without any ties. It was worlds away from the life she had once envisaged for herself.

She ran herself a bath and lay in the foamy water while her mind drifted back and forth, between past and present. Seeing Sam again had unsettled her—it had awoken feelings she had kept securely locked away until now. Since their divorce, she hadn't been out with anyone else, hadn't had sex, and hadn't missed it either, yet all of a sudden her body ached for fulfilment.

She wanted to be held and touched. She wanted to be kissed and she wanted to feel alive again and not as though she was in a state of perpetual limbo. She wanted to experience passion again yet she knew that it wasn't as simple as finding someone she was attracted to and sleeping with him. It never had been. Before she could give herself to a man, she had to be in love with him, had to know that he loved her, too, and there was only one man she had ever felt like that about, and that was Sam.

Closing her eyes, she let her mind open to the memories, remembering how it had felt when he had held her, loved her, made her feel that she was the most important person in the world. Sam had loved her so much and she had driven him away. She may have had her reasons and they may have been the best reasons in the world, but as she lay there on her own in her lonely house, all Anna wanted was Sam there beside her, Sam loving her, Sam back in his rightful place, as the focus of her world, as she was the focus of his. And the hardest thing of all was knowing that she would never experience that kind of joy again.

It was six a.m. on a wet and dreary Sunday morning and Sam had just arrived for work. After a stint of nights he'd been rostered for the early shift over the weekend. He'd long since accepted that doing locum work meant that he drew the short straw when it came to the hours he worked so the rapid turn-around didn't bother him. After all, he had nothing better to do with his time.

He grimaced as he loped towards the main entrance to the hospital. There was no point getting maudlin. Maybe his life wasn't exactly a hotbed of excitement but he was very lucky to do a job he loved. Pushing open the heavy glass door, he strode into the foyer, only to grind to a halt when he almost mowed down the woman who was hurrying in the opposite direction. His heart ricocheted off a couple of his ribs when he realised it was Anna. It was an effort to behave as though nothing was amiss when what he wanted to do was haul her into his arms and kiss her until they were both senseless. However, he doubted if she would appreciate such tactics at this hour on a cold winter morning.

'Just going off duty?' he asked when she stopped, hoping he had managed to dredge up a suitably noncommittal expression.

'Just coming on, actually.' She sighed wearily. 'I got all the way upstairs and realised that I'd left my briefcase in the car so had to come back down to fetch it.'

'What a bind,' Sam said sympathetically, taking note of the inky shadows under her eyes. She looked completely worn out and he couldn't help wondering if it was just the pressure of work that was having such an effect on her, or if there was another reason for it.

He quickly dismissed the thought, refusing to delve any deeper for the sake of his sanity. Maybe Anna had spent some time thinking about him in the past few days but it didn't mean anything. He glanced over his shoulder and frowned when he saw that the rain had turned into a veritable deluge now.

'You'll get soaked if you go out in that downpour. Haven't you got an umbrella?'

'Yes, but it's in the car.'

She gave a little shrug and once again Sam was struck by the weariness that seemed to be emanating from her. Surely not even the fact that she did such a demanding job should have left her looking so drained, he thought.

'Give me your keys and I'll fetch your case for you,' he said, coming to a swift decision. He shook his head when she opened her mouth to protest. 'You may as well give in gracefully, Anna, because I'm not letting you go out in all that rain to get soaked.'

She gave a little moue of annoyance as she jiggled the keys in her hand. 'I'm not going to melt, Sam. Stop fussing.'

Sam didn't say anything. He merely held out his hand and after a moment's hesitation she dropped the keys into his palm. 'I've parked by the staff accommodation block—do you know where that is?'

'Yep,' he assured her, although he didn't have a clue. He pocketed the keys then pushed open the door. 'I'll bring your briefcase upstairs for you.'

'Thanks. I appreciate it.'

Sam smiled thinly as he stepped out into the downpour because it hadn't sounded as though she'd really meant that. However, the fact that she had given in after only a token protest proved how tired she was. Anna was working herself into the ground and it worried him to know how little care she took of herself. Maybe he could make her see that she needed to slow down?

The thought occupied him while he tracked down her car. Fortunately, it didn't take him long to find it but he was still wringing wet by the time he got back inside the hospital. He called into the ED first to let the staff know that he had arrived then went to the lift. He had his bleep switched on so if anything happened he could be back in the department within minutes.

The obs and gynae unit was fairly peaceful for once. With it being so early, most of the usual hustle and bustle hadn't begun. Sam headed to the office to find Anna but she wasn't there. He finally tracked her down in the ward kitchen, sipping a mug of steaming hot coffee as though her very life depended on it. She glanced up when she heard his footsteps and he saw panic flare in her eyes for a second before she hastily masked it.

'I see you found the car all right,' she said, glancing at her briefcase.

'Yes.' He placed the case on the table and handed back her keys.

'Thanks. I really appreciate this, Sam,' she said quietly, stowing the keys in her jacket pocket.

'No sweat,' he replied easily, and she chuckled.

'Where did you pick up that expression?'

'Oz.' Sam grinned as he hitched a hip onto the edge of the table. 'It's amazing how quickly you pick up the lingo. Another couple of months out there and you'd not have been able to tell me from a bona fide native.'

'I don't think so!' She laughed out loud, her face lighting up in a way that immediately made his heart start to bounce around inside his rib-cage again. Sam made a determined effort to control it. At this rate it was going to wear itself out.

'So you don't think I could hack it as a real, dyed-in-the-wool Ozzie?' he demanded, doing his best to sound affronted.

'No, I don't. I can't imagine you ever losing your Irish accent.'

'I don't have an accent!' he exclaimed in genuine surprise.

'Oh, yes you do.' She grinned at him. 'Maybe you can't hear it but other people can, believe me.'

'Really?' He pulled a face when she nodded. 'And here I was thinking that I spoke perfect Queen's English, too.'

'You do.' She chuckled impishly. 'You just speak it with a touch of the blarney.'

Sam shook his head in mock despair. 'I'm not sure if I like being on the receiving end of all these home truths. Is there anything else you feel the need to tell me? Don't be shy, Anna. I can take it.'

'No. That's all.'

She raised her cup and took a sip of the coffee. Sam sighed when he saw that the shutters had come down again. For a few minutes she had forgotten that she needed to be on her guard around him and he had enjoyed their exchange. It reminded him of all the other times they had poked gentle fun at each other.

That had been one of the best things about their relationship, he realised with a pang. They'd been able to laugh at one another as well as laugh together. They had trusted each other so completely that neither of them had felt the need to protect themselves. They had been a team, united against whatever life could throw at them. He had truly believed that their love had made them invincible.

It was simply too painful to remember how good his life had been at one point. Sam swung round and headed to the door. 'I'd better get back to ED before they send out a search party. I'll see you later, I expect.'

'I expect so. And thanks again, Sam, for doing your knight errant act. You always were the perfect gentleman.'

'That's me,' he said lightly, shooting her a grin before he beat a hasty retreat. He knew that if he lingered he might start to think that he was in with a chance, and that would be a very stupid thing to do for any number of reasons.

He made himself recite all the reasons why he and Anna could never get back together, starting with the main one, which was that they'd had their chance and failed. That should have been enough to convince him it would never happen, but he floundered through a couple more just to make sure: he didn't intend to risk having his heart broken all over again; they would still have to contend with the same issues about them being childless. However, even after dredging up all that, he still wasn't convinced. OK, so he was ninety-nine per cent certain that it wouldn't work, but there was still that one per cent niggling away at him: Anna wasn't indifferent to him and he most certainly wasn't indifferent to her. Surely that had to count for something. Didn't it?

CHAPTER FOUR

THE morning soon picked up after its unusually lei-
surely start. Anna was about to begin the ward round
when she received a message saying that one of her
mums was being brought in by ambulance. Leaving
her senior registrar, Pritti Patel, to take the round, she
hurried to the office and brought up the patient's file
on the computer.

At the age of forty-six, Helen Denning was one of
their older mums. Although the pregnancy had come as
a complete surprise to Helen and her husband, Brian,
the couple had been thrilled at the thought of them
having another child. Because of Helen's age, Anna had
recommended a whole battery of tests should be done
but nothing untoward had shown up. Now in her
seventh month, Helen had sailed through her pregnancy
so far and there was nothing in her file to indicate what
might have gone wrong at this point.

Anna left the office and went downstairs to meet the
ambulance. There was a separate entrance for the maternity unit so she keyed in the security code and
unlocked the door. By the time the ambulance arrived,

she had a porter standing by as well as Janet Clarke, the senior midwife on duty that day.

Anna listened carefully as the lead paramedic explained that Helen was bleeding heavily and in a great deal of pain as they unloaded the stretcher. He filled her in on the amount of fluid that had been administered and what pain relief the patient had received as well.

'Thank you. Take her straight through to the delivery room,' she instructed when he had finished.

She hurried along beside the stretcher as they rushed Helen down the corridor. 'You're going to be fine, Helen. We'll get you sorted out as quickly as we can.'

'What about the baby?' Helen pleaded. She grasped Anna's hand. 'You will help him, won't you, Dr Carter?'

'I'll do everything I can, Helen. I promise you.'

Anna squeezed her hand then had to let it go as they reached the delivery suite. The porter elbowed open the doors and the whole convoy swept into the room. Anna didn't waste any time as she issued instructions.

'I want her on the bed, stat. Bloods, BP, and sats need doing, and can you cross-match three litres of blood— her blood group is on file so that should help to speed things up.'

The midwife hurriedly started attaching Helen to the various pieces of monitoring equipment. Anna quickly set up the ultrasound scanner so she could establish what was going on. Once she had a better idea of the problem, she would know how to deal with it.

'Right, Helen, I'm going to do an ultrasound to see what's happening,' she explained, smearing jelly onto the patient's stomach. 'It's exactly the same as the other scans you've had done so there's no need to worry.'

'I can't feel the baby moving,' Helen gasped through her tears. 'Does that mean he's dead?'

'No. He's probably just lying still for a change,' Anna said soothingly as she ran the wand over Helen's tummy. She couldn't tell very much from her first sweep but a second one soon established what the problem was. Part of the placenta had become detached from the wall of the uterus and that was what was causing the bleeding.

'Is he all right?' Helen demanded, twisting round so she could see the screen.

'I'm just about to check that,' Anna explained, passing the wand over Helen's stomach once more and smiling when she saw the baby's arms moving. 'There he is now. Look, he's waving to you.'

She positioned the screen so that Helen could get a better look at her child then called Janet over. 'How's the baby doing?' she asked, *sotto voce,* so Helen couldn't overhear.

'Heartbeat is a little faster than normal but not worryingly so,' the midwife explained, showing Anna the printout from the foetal monitor.

Anna studied it for a second. 'I'm going to wait and see if the bleeding settles down then. So long as there's no immediate danger to the baby or to the mother, I won't intervene. Every extra day we can delay delivery increases the child's chances. I'm going to need someone in here to monitor the situation, though, so can you arrange that for me?'

'I'll try.' Janet grimaced. 'We're really short-staffed with it being so close to Christmas. I'm not sure if there's anyone to spare.'

Anna sighed. It was the same story every year. Staff wanted to be at home to enjoy the festivities with their families so there was always a lot of leave taken over the holiday period. 'See what you can do, Janet. If there's nobody available, I'll contact one of the agencies and see if they have anyone on their books.'

'You must be miracle worker if you can find any agency staff willing to work at this time of the year,' Janet replied cheerfully as she went to the phone.

Anna understood her scepticism. The chances of her finding someone willing to work in the run-up to Christmas was probably zero. Still, if all else failed then she would just have to do it herself, she decided as she told Helen what was happening. One thing was certain, though: she wasn't going to put her patients' lives at risk. If she had to work all through the holiday, that's what she would do. After all, she had nothing better planned. Christmas on her own wasn't the most appealing of prospects.

Just for a second her mind drifted back to the first Christmas she and Sam had spent together after they had married. They'd been living in a poky little flat in one of the dreariest parts of London at the time. They'd had very little money to spare and had agreed not to waste too much cash on decorating the place. Anna had bought a scrawny little tree from the local market and they'd spent one whole evening making decorations to hang on it. She smiled to herself as she remembered the star Sam had made out of a piece of cardboard covered with tinfoil. No matter how much they had twisted and turned it around, it had still ended up looking decidedly skew-whiff!

They'd also set a limit on the amount they could spend on presents for each other. Ten pounds and not a penny more had been the agreed sum. Anna had spent her share on some wool and had knitted Sam a scarf and, despite the odd dropped stitch, he'd been thrilled to bits. As he'd told her, it had been knitted with love and that was what had made it so special.

Her present had been equally beautiful—a necklace made out of shells they had gathered together one summer's day at the beach. The fact that Sam had taken so much time and trouble to polish the shells had made it more valuable to her than any amount of diamonds.

It had been the most wonderful Christmas Anna had ever had, and it was painful to recall how happy she had been at the time. She pushed the memory aside. Those days were long gone and there was no point looking back, no point at all.

'Right, then, can you tell me when this all started?'

Sam drew the curtain around the bed and turned to the young woman standing beside him. Jade Jackson had been less than helpful since she had brought her six-month-old daughter, Chantal, into ED. All she had told the triage nurse was that the baby had been screaming all night long, and it wasn't much to go on. Sam sensed that it would need a lot of patience get to the root of the problem and smiled at her.

'You told the nurse that Chantal had been screaming all last night. Is that right?'

'Yes,' Jade muttered, avoiding his eyes. With her thin legs sticking out from under a skimpy little miniskirt and her long hair hanging down her back, she looked little more than a child herself. At a rough guess, Sam would have said that she was in her mid-teens— certainly not much older—and she was obviously uncomfortable about having to deal with someone in authority.

'Babies tend to get a lot of wind at this age,' he observed with another soothing smile. He knew from experience that the key to making a speedy diagnosis was to get Mum on side as quickly as possible so he needed to reassure Jade that she wasn't in any trouble. 'It's often that which makes them cry such a lot, I find.'

'Tell me about it!' Jade grimaced. 'She's full of wind every time I feed her.'

Sam laughed. 'I can imagine,' he said, gently removing the baby's nappy. He carefully felt her tummy, murmuring to the poor little mite when she immediately started screaming again. 'It's OK, sweetheart. We'll soon have you feeling better.'

He turned to the mother again. 'Has Chantal been sick at all?'

'Yes. She was sick last night and again this morning,' Jade told him, looking scared to death. 'I just fed her as normal, though, so it couldn't have been anything I did.'

'I'm sure it wasn't,' Sam replied lightly, watching as the baby drew up her legs to her tummy—a classic sign of colic in an infant this age. He glanced at the nurse who was standing beside the bed. 'Can you take her temperature for me, please?'

He waited while the nurse checked Chantal's temperature, nodding when she told him it was normal. 'Well, it doesn't look as though Chantal's suffering from an infection of any sort.'

'So you think it's just wind?' Jade said eagerly. 'I told my mum that was all it was, but she insisted that I had to bring Chantal in to see you. She doesn't seem to think I can look after her properly, but I do my best.'

'I'm sure you do, Jade. I expect your mum was just concerned about her, and quite right, too. It's always better to err on the safe side with a baby this age so you mustn't worry about taking Chantal to see your GP or bringing her here even. Nobody's going to think that you've done something wrong. OK?'

'OK,' Jade agreed, looking a little happier after hearing that.

Sam picked up the baby's nappy, frowning when he saw that there was both blood and mucus in it. 'Have you seen this?' he asked, showing it to the girl.

'I changed her before we came out,' Jade said quickly.

'I meant the blood and that slimy stuff,' he explained mildly.

'Oh. Right. I see.' Jade bit her lip. 'There was some in her nappy last night but I didn't think it was important so that's why I didn't mention it.'

Sam stifled a sigh. The girl's parenting skills seemed sadly lacking from what he had seen so far. 'I know it's difficult looking after a baby, but something like this can be a sign that all isn't well. It's always safer to get it checked out.'

He turned to the nurse while Jade digested that piece of advice. 'I'd like a barium enema X-ray done. Can you phone the radiography unit and let them know? And tell them it's urgent. I don't want to hang around too long.'

The nurse hurried away as Sam sat the young mother down in a chair. 'Although it could turn out that Chantal just has a severe case of colic, there's a possibility that she's suffering from something called intussusception.'

'Intuss— What on earth is that?' Jade demanded, going white.

'It's a condition whereby part of the intestine telescopes in on itself,' he explained. 'The best way to explain it is to imagine what happens when you pull off a tightly fitting glove and part of the finger turns itself inside out. Sometimes the bowel can do that and I think it's possible that it's happened in this instance.'

'But Chantal was fine yesterday,' the young mother protested. 'She was a bit grouchy but she wasn't *ill!*'

'It can happen quite quickly. Nobody is really sure why it occurs either—it could be due to a recent infection or there could be a small polyp in the intestine which triggers it. However, if it is intussusception, it's extremely serious. In severe cases, the blood supply to the intestine is cut off and that can lead to gangrene.'

'But why do you think that's what's wrong with Chantal?'

'Because she is exhibiting all the classic symptoms.' He ticked them off on his fingers. 'Severe abdominal colic which makes the child scream intermittently. Vomiting, plus blood and mucus in the faeces.'

Jade's face crumpled. 'She's not going to die, is she? I couldn't bear it if anything happened to her.'

'Chantal is not going to die,' Sam said firmly. 'You've done exactly the right thing and brought her into the hospital, and now we shall treat her. I've ordered a barium enema X-ray and that will show if there is a blockage in her intestine.'

'And what happens if there is?' Jade asked, wiping her runny nose on her sleeve.

Sam handed her a tissue. 'Sometimes the enema itself can right the problem. It can force the intestine back into its proper place.'

'And if it doesn't work?'

'Then Chantal will need an operation to sort everything out,' he said gently.

'Oh!' The girl started wailing when she heard that. Sam sighed as he patted her hand.

'I know this must have been a shock for you, Jade. Would you like me to call your mum so she can be here with you?'

'Yes, please.'

Jade mopped her eyes then wrote down her home phone number and gave it to him. The nurse reappeared just then to tell him that the baby could be taken straight to the radiography unit. Sam summoned a porter then explained to Jade that she could go with her daughter and sent them on their way. He just had time to phone the grandmother and tell her what had happened before he was needed again.

This time it was a six-year-old boy who had fallen down the stairs and suffered a nasty concussion. As he arranged for a CT scan to be done, Sam couldn't help thinking that parenthood must be fraught with anxieties, not that he would ever experience it himself. The only woman he had wanted to have his children had been Anna, but it hadn't happened despite all the tests and treatment they had undergone.

The doctors had explained that because Anna had suffered from severe endometriosis her chances of conceiving had been very slim. The condition was caused when fragments of the endometrium—the lining of the uterus—travelled from the uterus into the pelvic cavity via the Fallopian tubes and attached themselves to other organs. These fragments continued to respond to the woman's menstrual cycle but as the blood failed to escape it caused the formation of cysts, and that was what was believed to have affected her fertility.

It had been hard for Sam to accept that he would never have the family he had dreamed of, but what had hurt him more was knowing how Anna had felt. She had been devastated by the prognosis and nothing he had said or done had made it any easier for her.

The truth was that although Anna had always been enough for him, he had never been enough for her: she'd needed children as well. No wonder his head was telling him there was no point even thinking about them trying again.

By the time lunchtime rolled around, Helen Denning's condition was starting to improve. Anna was quietly confident that they would be able to delay delivering the baby for a while longer if the placenta didn't detach itself any further. Janet had managed to persuade one of her staff to work overtime so at least Anna was sure that Helen would be properly monitored while she took a quick break.

She went to the staff canteen, groaning when she discovered there was a long queue at the counter. She was about to give it up as a bad job and settle for a chocolate bar from one of the vending machines when she saw Sam waving to her from the front of the line.

'What do you want?' he mouthed above everyone's heads.

'Er...um...anything at all,' Anna said, somewhat flummoxed by the question. She saw him lean over and pick up a dish from the hot plate before he went to the till, and sighed. She really didn't want to be away too long, but she could hardly leave now that it appeared Sam had bought her some lunch.

He eased his way past the queue and stopped beside her. 'I got you some lasagne. I hope that's all right.'

'Yes, it's fine. Here, let me pay you for it.' Anna went to open her purse but he shook his head.

'A portion of lasagne isn't going to break the bank... Oh, great, there's someone leaving. Get a move on, Anna, and grab that table before someone else gets there before us. Quick!'

Before she realised what she was doing, Anna found herself responding to the instruction. Hurrying across the canteen, she plonked herself down at the table then flushed when she realised how undignified she must have looked.

'Good to see you can still show a clean pair of heels when you have to.' Sam placed the tray on the table and grinned at her, his green eyes sparkling with laughter, and Anna felt another tide of heat assail her.

She hurriedly looked away, not proof against the feelings that were running riot inside her all of a sudden. So maybe Sam was an extremely handsome man, and maybe she did still find him attractive, but none of that mattered. It was just a physical response which she would regret to her dying day if she acted on it.

She'd been there, done that, bought the T-shirt *and* discarded it, and she wasn't about to make the mistake of thinking they could pick up where they had left off. She and Sam Kearney were history. The last chapter of their marriage had been written three years ago and there wasn't going to be an epilogue. Not even for sex. Not even for *wonderful* sex!

Anna gasped as the thought appeared from nowhere, or was it really from nowhere? Hadn't she been thinking about sex and Sam for several days, remembering how it had felt to have him hold her, love her, make her body burn with desire? Night after night, she'd lain awake, torturing herself with both the memories and her fantasies. No wonder she was so worn out, so on edge, so… so *frustrated*. She wanted to sleep with Sam again and she wanted to do it sooner rather than later because if she had to wait then she might just go stark raving mad!

'Anna? Hey, what is it? What's wrong?'

Anna almost leapt six feet into the air when Sam jogged her arm. It was only the fact that she was wedged against the wall that kept her grounded, in fact.

Her heart was racing away inside her, making it impossible to speak as the blood whooshed through her veins. All she could do was stare dumbly back at him.

'I don't know what's going on inside your head, Anna, but whatever it is, you can tell me about it.'

Sam leant forward until his face blotted out everything else. Anna gulped. Now that she could no longer see the rest of the people in the canteen, it was harder than ever to control her emotions. She had to force herself to remember where they were and not let herself get carried away to that fantasy world of her own making.

A groan escaped her as the images that had plagued her for days came rushing back. She could almost feel Sam touching her, stroking her, bringing her body to life….

'Anna, sweetheart, what *is* it?'

The feel of Sam's hand on hers should have been the wake-up call she needed, but it wasn't. It blended so perfectly with her fantasy that she smiled. That was good. It proved he was in this with her…

'I think you should eat something.' Sam briskly withdrew his hand and Anna blinked as a fork suddenly appeared in its place. He pushed the plate of food towards her. 'Come on. There's nothing worse than cold pasta.'

Anna stared at the shiny metal implement she was clutching, scarcely able to believe what had happened. Had she really been on the verge of inviting Sam to make love to her right here in the middle of the staff canteen?

The heat she'd felt before was nothing to what she felt at that moment as her whole body suddenly burned with shame. Digging the fork into the pasta, she scooped up a chunk and shovelled it into her mouth. It could have been ambrosia or arsenic for all she cared because food was the last thing on her mind. What was uppermost was this fear that was uncoiling inside her, a fear of making a mistake she would regret to the end of her days. She might still want Sam but she must never let him know that. She had found the strength to let him go once before, but she knew that she wouldn't be able to find it again.

It had taken her years to come to terms with what had happened that night three years ago. The memory of Sam's expression when she had told him that she no longer wanted them to be man and wife had tormented her, day in and day out. Even though they had been going through a very difficult time, she knew that Sam had never expected her to reach such a decision.

He had pleaded with her to change her mind, begged her to reconsider and give them another chance, but she had held fast. Even when he had broken down and cried, she had managed to hold firm, sure in her own mind that she'd been doing the right thing, the *only* thing that would protect Sam's future happiness. However, that had been then and this was now, and she knew in her heart that if she let Sam make love to her now, she would beg him to stay with her and that it would ruin his life.

Tears stung her eyes but she blinked them away. The truth was that Sam deserved so much more than she could give him. He deserved a *real* woman, not some-one like her. Oh, she might look like a woman on the outside, but inside, where it really mattered, she was a mess. Sam needed a woman who could give him children and that was the one thing she couldn't do. She was barren.

CHAPTER FIVE

SAM literally had to force himself to put the food into his mouth. He had no idea what was going through Anna's head at that moment but the expression on her beautiful face made him want to weep.

He swallowed the mouthful of food, hoping he wouldn't throw up. Part of him wanted to know why she looked so devastated, yet another, more cowardly part, was afraid to ask her. He really wasn't sure if he could handle any major revelations at the moment.

The sound of his bleep going off broke the spell. He could barely contain his relief as he dug it out of his pocket and checked the display. 'ED,' he announced, hoping Anna couldn't tell how thankful he was to have an excuse to leave. 'Sorry, but I'm going to have to cut and run.'

'Don't worry about it.' She summoned a smile which didn't reach her eyes. 'I'll have to get back, too. I haven't got time to linger over lunch today.'

Sam frowned as he stood up and piled his dishes onto the tray. 'You've only been here for a few minutes. Surely the department can manage without you for a bit longer?'

'I wish.' She stood up as well. 'We're short-staffed with it being so close to Christmas and it's all hands to the pump, so to speak.'

'It's not good for you to work so hard,' Sam admonished as he followed her to the hatch.

'I don't work any harder than anyone else in this hospital,' she assured him, depositing her plate in the rack.

'No? So how come you look so worn out?' he challenged, following suit.

'Maybe age is catching up with me,' she retorted, heading for the door.

Sam laughed as he trailed her into the corridor. 'Anna, you're only thirty-five.'

'Thank you for reminding me.' She jabbed a finger on the button to summon the lift and Sam sighed. He wasn't sure why she was so touchy all of a sudden, but he decided that it might be diplomatic to change the subject.

'I had one of your mums in earlier,' he told her, leaning against the wall while they waited for the lift to arrive. 'Jade Jackson—do you remember her?'

'Of course, I do,' she replied sharply.

Sam didn't say anything, although he found it puzzling that she had taken offence at him mentioning her age. Anna wasn't vain. She never had been. Even though she had always attracted a lot of attention from the opposite sex, she had never let it go to her head. It had been one of the things he had loved most about her, in fact. She'd accepted that men had found her attractive and had never played on the fact. So how come she was so sensitive about her age all of a sudden? Had it anything to do with the fact that she had expected to have a family by this point in her life?

Sam sensed it was so and his heart ached for her. It was hard to hide his feelings but he knew she wouldn't thank him if he sympathised with her. 'Of course you do. Anyway, Jade brought in her daughter. It looks as though the poor little mite has an intussusception.'

'Really? So what have you done about it?' Anna asked in obvious concern.

'I've sent Chantal for a barium enema X-ray to check if I'm right first of all,' he replied, straightening up as the lift arrived. Anna stepped in and pressed the button for the ground floor as well as the third floor then glanced at him.

'And if you are right, then what? Will the baby need an operation?'

'We could be lucky and the enema will resolve the problem. However, if it doesn't then I'll admit Chantal to Paediatrics.' He grimaced. 'Jade was really upset when I explained it all to her.'

'She's a good kid, really,' Anna assured him. 'I know she comes across as a big dizzy but she's not had an easy time of it. She was barely sixteen when Chantal was born and the baby's father had disappeared off the scene way before then.'

'I didn't think she was very old.' Sam sighed. 'It's a lot to take on at her age, isn't it? Bringing up a child is a huge responsibility even for an adult.'

'It is, but I'm sure Jade did the right thing by keeping Chantal. I know her parents wanted her to have the baby adopted after it was born, but Jade would have regretted it if she'd given Chantal away.'

'What about the baby, though?' Sam said slowly. 'Do you think she would have been better off if she'd been adopted? I know Jade loves her but she doesn't seem to have much of a clue about looking after her.'

'No, I don't. Jade may not have any experience of looking after a child but she'll soon learn. And, as you said yourself, she really loves that little girl and that's what matters most of all in my opinion.'

They reached the third floor and the lift slowed to a stop. Sam put out his hand when Anna went to get out. He knew that he should be playing it safe by keeping his thoughts focused on the present but he couldn't resist harking back to the past again.

'We never did consider the idea of adopting a child, did we?'

'No, we didn't.' Anna's tone was bleak.

'Do you think that was a mistake?'

'I don't know.' She lifted sad eyes to his face. 'At the time, I just wanted to put an end to all the heartache we'd suffered. I don't think I could have gone through the strain of wondering if we would be accepted for adoption as well.'

'Me neither,' he said softly, his heart aching even more as he thought about everything she had been through. Not only had Anna had to contend with all the various tests and procedures, she'd also had to deal with the fact that she might never be able to conceive. It must have been incredibly difficult for her, and it was that thought that prompted him to do something he knew in his heart he really shouldn't do.

Leaning forward, he dropped a gentle kiss on her

lips. Her mouth was warm under his and so deliciously soft that his senses whirled. Kissing Anna had always been a delight and that hadn't changed. At one point he had planned his whole future on the taste and feel of her lips, but he couldn't do it again. He drew back, praying that she couldn't tell how much it hurt to know that he had lost the most precious thing he would ever have in his life.

'I'm so sorry, Anna. About everything that happened.'

'I am, too,' she whispered as she stepped around him.

Sam leant against the wall as the doors closed, feeling the agony burning deep into his soul. He wanted to go after her and tell her that he could make things right if she would let him, but it would be an empty promise, one without any substance. He couldn't heal her broken heart because he couldn't give her what she wanted most of all—a baby. No matter what he said or did, he could never make her life complete. She would always feel this sadness, always weep inside for the child she couldn't have, and he didn't think he could bear to watch her suffer again.

The doors opened and the noise of a busy emergency department came flooding into the lift, drowning out his thoughts and providing him with a welcome distraction. As he headed to Resus, Sam gave thanks once again for the fact that he had a job that demanded all his attention. At least while he was working he could escape from the memories of the past, and as long as he didn't add to them by making more while he was here in Dalverston, he would survive.

If only he could be sure that Anna would get over what had happened eventually, he would feel so much better, but he doubted if she ever would. Some wounds were just too deep to heal.

By the time six p.m. came around, Anna was flagging. She should have gone off duty several hours before but there'd been no chance of that. There had been a number of emergency cases that day and each one had demanded her full concentration. As she left Theatre after a particularly difficult delivery, she could feel her head reeling with tiredness but her day wasn't over yet. She still had to speak to the patient's husband and make sure he understood what had happened.

She discarded her gown then went to the relatives' room. The poor man looked almost as exhausted as she felt as he paced the floor. He spun round when he heard the door open and Anna hastened to reassure him when she saw the fear on his face.

'Congratulations, Mr Graham, you have healthy baby girl. You'll be able to see her and your wife just as soon as Denise comes round from the anaesthetic.'

'A girl!' His mouth dropped open as he starred at Anna in confusion. 'But I thought we were going to have a boy this time. I don't know what we're going to do now. I mean, we haven't even *thought* about any girls' names.'

'Why don't we sit down?' Anna said firmly, discarding any thoughts she'd had about making the announcement and slipping away.

She sighed as she led the new father to a chair because she'd seen this reaction before. People got it into their heads that they were having either a boy or a girl and were stunned when the baby turned out to be the other gender. Some were so disappointed that it stopped them bonding with their child and she was determined that it wasn't going to happen in this instance. One thing she and Sam had agreed on from the moment they'd decided to try for a baby had been that they hadn't cared what sex it would be. So long as the child was healthy, that had been all that had mattered.

Anna bit her lip as stabbing pain pierced her heart. It was an effort to focus when she could feel her emotions welling up inside her once more. Seeing Sam again seemed to have unloosed all the feelings she'd kept locked away these past three years and now they threatened to overwhelm her. It was only the fact that she had a job to do that kept her focused, in fact.

'As you know, the baby was lying horizontally in the womb, which was why it was necessary to perform a Caesarean section,' she began, hoping it would help if she talked the father through the whole procedure. 'When a baby is lying in that position, it's impossible to deliver it vaginally as the arm and the shoulder can become jammed in the pelvis.'

'I understand, Dr Carter.' Alistair Graham nodded. He seemed a little calmer now that he was getting over his initial shock. 'I know that Denise really wanted to have a natural birth but there was no chance of that, was there?'

'No,' Anna concurred. 'Our main concern always has to be the safety of the mother and the child.

Although your wife may be disappointed about us having to intervene, it was absolutely essential.'

'I'm sure Denise realises that.' He gave Anna a rather sheepish smile. 'You must think I'm a real idiot for blathering on like that about us not having chosen any girls' names.'

'Not at all.' Anna laughed, relieved that he seemed to be rallying so well. 'Believe me, Mr Graham, you aren't the first shocked father I've seen, neither will you be the last.' She stood up. 'One of the nurses will fetch you as soon as your wife has recovered. I'll be here for a little while longer so if there's anything else you want to know, just ask one of the staff to call me.'

Anna left the room and went to check on her patient. Denise had come round from the anaesthetic and was happily cuddling her new little daughter. Anna had a word with her and made sure there were no problems then told the nurse that she could fetch Mr Graham in. Once that was done, technically she was free to leave, but before she went home she wanted to make a final check on Helen Denning.

It was gone seven before Anna finally left work and the staff car park was half empty. She unlocked her car and tossed her briefcase onto the back seat then slid behind the wheel. Slotting the key into the ignition, she switched on the engine and groaned when nothing happened. Of all the days for the car to start playing up!

She tried to start it a couple more times then gave up. She knew absolutely nothing about engines so there was no point looking under the bonnet. She would have to phone for a taxi and arrange for the local garage to collect the car when she got home.

She took her briefcase off the back seat and hunted out her mobile phone, closing her eyes in despair when she discovered that the battery was flat. Now she would have to trail all the way back to her office and phone for a cab from there.

She was just crossing the car park when a car drew up beside her and she sighed when she realised it was Sam. Her emotions had been in turmoil ever since lunchtime and she could have done with a bit more breathing space before she had to speak to him again. He was obviously surprised to see her because he was frowning as he rolled down the window.

'I thought you'd have gone home ages ago.'

'I had a couple of emergency cases and they delayed me,' she replied, without breaking stride.

'I see.' He let the car crawl along beside her. 'How come you're heading back into work, though? Did you forget something?'

Anna shook her head, loath to explain that her car had broken down and that she was stranded when she knew what would happen. Sam would offer her a lift home and she wasn't sure if she could cope with spending any more time with him at the present moment.

'The battery on my mobile's flat and I need to make a phone call,' she explained ambiguously.

'Use mine.' Sam brought the car to a halt and lifted his phone out of the cradle on the dashboard. He offered it to her. 'Here you go.'

'I…um…' Anna knew she was stuck then. The moment Sam heard her order a taxi, he would be bound to step in. She sighed under her breath. It would be quicker and easier to tell him the truth and get it over with. 'I was going to phone for a taxi because my car won't start.'

'And you thought it best not to tell me what had happened in case I offered to run you home?'

His voice was level enough but she saw the hurt in his eyes and knew she couldn't make matters worse by lying to him. 'Yes.'

He shook his head. 'I'm not trying to make life difficult for you, Anna. It's the last thing I want to do.'

'I know that,' she said quickly, then shrugged when he looked at her in disbelief. 'I do, Sam. And it's not you, or at least it's not anything you've said or done. It's me. I just feel very…well, *unsettled* at the moment with seeing you again.'

'I understand, Anna. Really I do. I feel exactly the same if it's any consolation.'

'Do you?' She was unable to hide her surprise and he smiled ruefully.

'Yes. I know it's been three years and that I shouldn't feel so on edge, but I do. We went through such a lot together, and I don't just mean when we were trying for a baby either. We had good times as well as bad, and I can't help thinking about all that when we're together, even though I know it's all in the past.'

'It's the same for me,' she admitted softly.

'Then why don't we accept it and stop trying to pretend that we're indifferent to one another? I care about you, Anna. I always have and I always will, but I know that we can't be anything more than friends now. If you're worried in case I'm going to try to persuade you to come back to me then, please, don't be.' He shrugged. 'We both know it wouldn't work so let's just enjoy what we have.'

'And what's that?' she asked, forcing the words past the lump that had suddenly formed in her throat. There was no point feeling hurt about what Sam had said, no point at all wishing that he *had* wanted her to go back to him when she knew as well as he did that it could never work. She should just be grateful for the fact that he felt able to be so honest with her about his feelings.

'Friendship. You know me better than anyone else in the whole wide world. I don't need to pretend with you, Anna. I can be myself, warts and all.'

He took a deep breath but she could hear the tension in his voice when he continued and knew how much it was costing him to say this to her.

'What we have is something really special, something I don't want to lose again. Do you?'

CHAPTER SIX

'THIS is really lovely. You've done a brilliant job in here, Anna.'

Sam smiled as he looked around the ground-floor living area of Anna's house. The fact that she had agreed to let him drive her home had proved that he'd been right to be so open about his feelings with her. At the time he'd wondered if he'd been making a mistake but now he was sure it had been the right thing to do. They needed to lay the foundations for their new relationship so that they could relax and enjoy it. Hopefully, he had taken the first step towards achieving that.

'Thank you. The place was a mess when I bought it. Everywhere was damp and covered in mildew. I didn't think I'd ever get rid of the musty smell!'

She laughed, obviously pleased by his reaction, and Sam felt his spirits lift that bit further. This was easier than he'd feared it would be and if they carried on this way there shouldn't be any problems at all. He crossed the living room and studied the glossy white kitchen cabinets, closing his mind to the memory of the poky little kitchen they'd had in their first home. He mustn't keep looking back. He had to move forward and enjoy this new relationship they had.

'I love the kitchen. It looks like something out of one of those ideal-homes magazines—all glossy and oozing style.'

'It's really practical too,' Anna said firmly, coming to join him. 'There's loads of storage space, which is an absolute must in a house this small.'

'Better than having to store half your utensils in cardboard boxes under the sink because there's no-where else to put them,' he said without thinking, then could have bitten off his tongue at the lapse. Hadn't he just sworn there would be no more looking back, so why on earth had he said that?

'Like in our first flat?' Anna laughed but he could hear the edge in her voice even though she tried to hide it.

'Uh-huh,' he said, hoping to skate over the crack that had suddenly appeared beneath him. It made him see that he would need to be far more careful, at least for a while. Once they had settled into their roles as friends, it was bound to get easier, but for the moment he needed to think first and speak second.

'Why don't you have a look upstairs while I make some coffee?' Anna suggested. She filled the coffee-maker with water then glanced at him when he hesitated. 'Go on. I know you're dying to look around.'

Sam grimaced. 'Is it that obvious?' He chuckled when she arched a brow. 'OK, then. I don't need to be told twice.'

He left the living room and climbed the steep stairs

to the first floor. There was a tiny landing at the top with just two doors opening off it. Sam opened the door on his left first and whistled under his breath when he saw the luxurious bathroom with its gleaming porcelain fittings and creamy marble tiles on the walls and the floor.

Closing the bathroom door, he opened the second door and felt his breath catch when he found himself standing on the threshold of Anna's bedroom. She'd used the same neutral colours in here, too, but had added touches of chocolate-brown this time—a mound of chocolate brown satin pillows and a matching throw on the double bed, a brown silk robe lying over the back of a rattan chair.

Sam felt his stomach perform a somersault as he pictured Anna slipping off the robe and lying down on the bed. The colour of the pillows would be an almost perfect match for her hair. He could imagine himself lying down beside her while he pulled out the pins and spread the gleaming strands over that slippery, glossy satin...

He took a deep breath and closed the door, not proof against the feelings that were running riot inside him. He couldn't afford to indulge in that kind of thinking if he was to make their new relationship work.

Anna had the coffee ready when he went back downstairs. Sam took the mug she offered him and inhaled appreciatively, hoping the caffeine would steady his nerves.

'That smells good,' he said with determined bonhomie. 'My taste buds are in revolt after being forced to drink that disgusting brew they serve in the canteen.'

'You and your coffee!' She laughed as she kicked off her shoes and curled up in a chair. 'You always were faddy about it.'

'Faddy?' Sam did his best to look hurt. It wasn't difficult because there was an ache in his gut which was in danger of taking over completely if he wasn't careful. He and Anna were *not* going to lie together in that bed and he had to accept that and stop whinging! 'Just because I expect coffee to *taste* like coffee doesn't make me faddy.'

'If you say so,' she agreed, rolling her eyes.

Sam laughed. 'OK, so maybe I am a bit of pain when it comes to the perfect cup of coffee, but it's my only foible.'

'Really?' She didn't try to hide her scepticism this time. 'What about the fact that you loathe any fancy sauces on your food? And that you hate it when the vegetables come pared into those fancy little shapes?'

'Can I help it if I like my food to look like food and not like a work of art?' he countered. 'Anyway, I'm not the only one around here who has little quirks when it comes to food. It wasn't me who had near hysterics when she found out that she'd eaten an oyster, was it?'

'Do you blame me?' Anna shuddered. 'Just thinking about it makes me feel queasy. Yuck!'

'I rest my case.'

Sam sipped his coffee, enjoying the easy rapport that seemed to be developing between them. It had been like this when they had first got married, he thought wistfully. They had enjoyed each other's company so much that they had rarely felt the need to go out and socialise. So much of their time had been taken up by work that the hours they'd had together had been too precious to waste.

His mind skated back over lazy evenings spent in front of the television or reading. They'd enjoyed simple pleasures and never hankered after the high life. Even when they had gone out, it had been very low-key—drinks with friends, a meal at the local bistro. Their tastes had been so in tune and it was good to discover that they still got on so well together even though the situation was very different today.

'What are your lodgings like?' Anna suddenly asked. 'Did your landlady turn out to be a dragon as you feared she might be?'

'No, she's very nice, actually. She's a widow with a couple of grown-up children who live in London. I think she takes in lodgers as much for the company as for the extra money it brings in.'

Sam rested his head against the cushion. It had been a long day and tiredness was catching up with him but he felt far too comfortable to move just yet. He glanced at the clock on the mantelpiece and decided that he would allow himself another few minutes before he made tracks for home.

'Good. At least you have somewhere decent to stay, although I still don't understand why you didn't rent a flat while you were here.'

'It was too much hassle, as I explained,' he said lightly. 'I find it easier to stay at a B&B or in lodgings rather than go through all the rigmarole of signing a lease. This way, if I don't like where I'm working, I can up sticks and move on.'

'You must have a permanent place to live, though, don't you?' Anna queried, frowning.

Sam shook his head. 'Nope.'

He sighed when he saw her surprise. He really didn't want to explain his aversion to putting down roots in case she guessed that it was because of what had happened between them, but now he had got this far, he had no choice.

'I just never wanted to stay in any one place for very long after the divorce so it was pointless finding myself a base when I wasn't going to be there. This way is much easier.'

'I'm so sorry, Sam.' Her voice caught. 'I never meant this to happen. It breaks my heart to think of you wandering about without a proper home to go back to.'

'I am perfectly happy with my life the way it is,' he said firmly even if it wasn't the truth. Granted, he enjoyed his job and was more than happy to move around while he was doing it, but his life certainly wasn't perfect. He closed his mind to the thought of what would help to make it perfect and carried on. 'I enjoy the freedom I have to come and go as I choose. If I want to work abroad, like that stint I did with the Flying Doctor Service in Australia, I can go and do it. I don't need to spend months sorting out my affairs and making provision for being away.'

'Obviously, you prefer not to be tied down,' she said slowly.

Sam frowned when he heard the edge in her voice.

'Yes, I suppose I do,' he agreed, because he was too busy working out what had caused it to consider what he was saying.

Anna gave him a tight little smile. 'Then maybe it's a good job we split up, don't you think?'

'I'm not sure I follow you,' he said, floundering a little.

'Oh, come on, Sam! You've just admitted that you enjoy the fact that you're no longer tied down, so why not admit that it was a relief when we got divorced? You regained your freedom, and that's what you really wanted, wasn't it?'

'That wasn't what I meant,' he said hotly.

'No?'

Scepticism oozed out of her and all of a sudden he couldn't take any more. Did she honestly believe that he had valued his freedom more than what they'd had? If she did then obviously she didn't understand him!

He stood up abruptly, incredibly hurt by the thought of how badly Anna had misjudged him. He would have given anything to save their marriage, done anything at all to make it work, but the truth was that nothing he could have done would have stopped them breaking up. Anna hadn't *really* wanted him—she'd wanted his baby. He had never been enough for her and he never would be. How foolish he'd been to imagine she had loved him as much as he had loved her.

'I think it's time I went home,' he said quietly, determined that he wasn't going to be drawn into an argument. He placed his cup on the table and went to the door. 'Thanks for the coffee. I'll see myself out.'

'I'm sorry, Sam. That was very unfair of me.'

Sam paused when he heard the catch in her voice, although he didn't look back. He was afraid of what Anna might see on his face if he did so. He really couldn't bear it if she knew how vulnerable he was, couldn't stand it if he made an even bigger fool of himself. 'It doesn't matter.'

'It does matter, though. I…I know how hard you fought to keep us together.'

'Do you? Do you really, Anna?' He swung round, needing to know if she was telling him the truth. His heart lurched when he saw the sorrow in her eyes because it was all too clear that she'd meant what she'd said.

'Yes. If you'd had your way we would still be married, Sam. It was me who pushed for a divorce, not you.'

'I always believed we could work through it,' he said roughly. 'I thought if we could get over the worst, we would find a way to rebuild our life together.'

'I know you did.' Tears sparkled in her eyes as she looked at him. 'But it wouldn't have been right, Sam. It wouldn't have been fair. Not to you.'

'What do you mean?' he demanded. He crossed the room and stood in front of her, feeling his head swirl as he stared into her eyes and saw the pain they held. 'Why wouldn't it have been fair to me specifically? We were married, Anna. What affected one of us affected us both.'

She started shaking her head before he had finished speaking. 'No, that isn't true. You're capable of fathering a child, Sam. All the tests we had done proved that conclusively. It's me who has the problem, not you. It wasn't fair that you should miss out because of my... failings.'

'Failings?' he repeated, stunned by what he was hearing. Reaching out he grasped her arms. 'You didn't fail at anything, Anna! It wasn't your fault that you couldn't have a baby. It was just one of those things that happens to some couples.'

'It's so typical of you to say that, Sam, but it isn't true. If you'd married someone else, you'd have had a child by now, maybe a couple of children—who knows?' She gave him a brave little smile and it almost tore his heart into two when he saw how her lips quivered.

'I didn't want anyone else,' he said softly, his eyes holding hers so that she would see he was telling her the truth. 'It was you I loved, Anna. Only you.'

She closed her eyes and he heard her take a shuddering breath as though she was drawing in the words and storing them deep inside her. The thought moved him so much that he gathered her into his arms and held her tightly against him. Her body felt so familiar as it nestled against his; he knew every curve and dip, recognised it with his heart as well as his mind. It was like coming home after a long and lonely journey, and the thought was just too much when his emotions were so raw.

Dipping his head, he kissed her with all the loneliness and despair that had been pent up inside him for the past three years. How many times had he dreamed of doing this, holding her, kissing her, losing himself in her sweetness? He'd lost count as well as lost all hope of it ever happening, yet it was happening now. Anna was here. She was in his arms, her heart beating under his, her breath mingling with his, and it felt like heaven. It was as though he had found his way back from the wilderness into the warmth and the light.

Tears filled his eyes and ran unheeded down his face as he kissed her again, softly, gently and with a passion he had never thought he would experience again. It was only Anna who could touch him this deeply, only Anna he had wanted this much; it was only Anna who could heal the wounds and make him feel whole again.

'Sam...don't. Please. You mustn't.... We mustn't.'

Her voice sounded as soft as a breeze even though the words weren't ones he wanted to hear. Sam didn't want to stop, didn't want to think if what he was doing was right, didn't want anything to take away the light and plunge him back into darkness. He pressed his lips to hers again, kissing her with an urgency he couldn't control, feeling the way she trembled as she tried to hold onto reason...

Her lips suddenly softened and clung to his, both giving and inviting a response, and joy surged through him. Now Anna was kissing *him*, holding *him* as close as he was holding her. When he ran his hand down her back, she whimpered, then did the same to him, her fingers trailing over the taut muscles, testing, feeling, relearning every plane and hollow. They were both breathless when they broke apart, both trembling, both aware that they were on the verge of something neither had expected to happen. Even though Sam knew it was what he wanted more than anything in the world, he also knew that Anna had to decide if it was right for her too.

He framed her face between his hands, his insides churning as fear claimed him. If she said no, that would be the end because he would accept her decision without question. He would never do anything that Anna might later regret. 'If this isn't what you want then say so. I'll understand, Anna. I swear I will. Just tell me to stop and that's it. It's over.'

'I don't want you to stop, Sam.' Her voice was firm and clear. It rang around the room and startled them both but she didn't flinch. 'I've wanted to make love with you from the first moment I saw you again.'

The admission was more than he had expected and more than he could deal with, to be honest. He'd been determined to keep his feelings in check since they had met and had assumed that Anna had felt exactly the same as him. To suddenly discover that she'd been thinking about them making love stunned him.

'Are you sure?' He took a steadying breath but his mind was reeling at the thought of Anna secretly harbouring this longing for him.

'Quite sure.' She looked into his eyes and he could see the certainty in her gaze. 'I won't regret it in the morning, Sam. I promise you that.'

'Sweetheart…!'

Her honesty moved him more than anything had ever done. As he pulled her back into his arms, Sam swore that, no matter what happened tomorrow, he would make this night special for her. It would be the most magical night of their lives, a night they would always remember.

He kissed her long and hungrily, feeling his passion surge when he felt her respond with equal ardour. When she wound her arms around his neck and drew his head down so she could deepen the kiss, he thought he was going to explode. It had been a long time since he had made love with a woman and this wasn't just any woman but Anna, the woman he had loved. The woman he loved still.

The thought wiped away any lingering doubts he might have had about the sense of what they were doing. Lifting her into his arms, he carried her up the stairs to the bedroom and laid her down on the bed. Switching on the bedside lamps, he smiled down at her.

'Will you be angry if I tell you that I pictured doing this very same thing when I was looking around the house earlier on tonight?'

'No, so long as you promise not to be angry if I tell you that I've thought about it happening a lot these past few days,' she murmured, smiling up at him.

Sam shuddered. 'I don't know what to say.'

'I don't think you need to say anything.' She took his hand and raised it to her lips. 'I want us to make love, Sam. Maybe I shouldn't have told you that, but I can't see any point in lying, can you?'

'No,' he said softly, humbly.

He turned her hand over and kissed her fingers, one by one, and felt her tremble. Placing her hand by her side, he turned his attention to the buttons on her blouse, his own hands shaking as he worked them free. Anna didn't say a word. She just lay there, her face looking so serene and so beautiful in the soft light that he was overwhelmed with emotion.

Bending down, he kissed her on the mouth, his lips lingering only long enough to draw a response from her before he straightened and continued his self-appointed task. Her skin was milky pale, soft and warm when his fingers brushed against it, and he drew in a ragged breath. He remembered how her skin had felt, remembered her scent, her taste, her softness, and it was hard to separate the memories from the reality of what was happening. For a moment he was afraid in case the present didn't live up to the past, but when the last button had been undone, and he saw the gentle swell of her breasts, he realised how foolish he had been to worry.

Nothing had changed. Three years may have passed but his feelings for her hadn't diminished. It was Anna he had wanted then and it was Anna, lying here before him, whom he wanted now. Nothing else mattered because it was Anna he loved.

CHAPTER SEVEN

ANNA CLOSED HER eyes as a wave of passion claimed her. Sam was stroking her breasts now, his touch so gentle that it felt as though she had stepped into one of her own fantasies. However, the feelings he was arousing inside her were far too real to be the figment of her imagination.

She smiled as her own fingers traced the strong line of his neck. He was still fully dressed but she managed to ease her fingertips inside the collar of his shirt. His skin was so warm, so smooth, so vital that she shivered.

She'd always loved the feel of his strong body, always enjoyed touching him. Making love with Sam had felt so right and so natural that she'd never had any inhibitions even though she'd had little experience before they'd met. After they had married they had made love whenever and wherever they had felt like it, enjoying each other's bodies and the pleasure they had given one another. It had only been later, once all the tests and procedures had begun, that the spontaneity had stopped. They'd been too consumed with the idea of trying to conceive a child to enjoy making love purely for the sake of it.

Sadness welled up inside her as she realised what they had lost. It hadn't been just a much-wanted child but part of themselves as well. She had never felt closer to any person than she'd felt to Sam when they had made love, and she regretted losing that intimacy now.

'Are you all right?'

Sam's voice was gentle as he turned her face towards him and she sighed. He'd always been an intuitive lover, able to read and react to her moods, and that hadn't changed.

'I was just thinking about how everything changed after all those tests we had.'

'Making love became a means to an end rather than an expression of our feelings for each other,' he said softly, and she nodded.

'Yes. I'm sorry, Sam. It was my fault…'

'No.' He stopped her with a gentle kiss. 'It wasn't anyone's fault, Anna. It just happened. You weren't to blame in any way at all.'

Her eyes filled with tears but before they could fall he kissed her again and kept on kissing her until her sadness was replaced by desire. Anna clung to him as he murmured soft words of endearment to her while he trailed kisses down her throat and across the swell of her breasts. When he took her nipple into his mouth and suckled her, she cried out, unable to hold back the tide of passion that was claiming her.

He stood up and stripped off his own clothes then removed the rest of hers before he lay down beside her again. Propping himself up on his elbow, he slid his hand beneath her head and started to pull out the hairpins.

'I stood in the doorway earlier and imagined how beautiful your hair would look spread across these pillows,' he told her, his eyes so dark a green that they appeared almost black. He ran his fingers through her hair then draped it over the satin pillow. 'I was right, too. It looks wonderful.'

Anna shuddered. In her mind's eye she could picture him standing on the threshold of her bedroom, and it was the most erotic experience to find herself in the midst of his fantasy. She ran a gentle hand down his face, letting her fingers follow the curve of his brow, the straight line of his nose, the firmness of his jaw. His face was as familiar to her as her own but she still enjoyed memorising its contours. One finger moved lazily around the chiselled perfection of his Cupid's-bow. Sam's mouth was perfect, not too big, not too small, just right...

Reaching up, she kissed him, wanting to taste as well as feel the perfection of those masculine lips. His response was immediate as he gathered her close so that her breasts were crushed against the hardness of his chest. Anna gasped when she felt the faint rasp of body hair on her sensitised nipples. It had been such a long time since she'd been naked in Sam's arms and she had forgotten how truly wonderful the experience could be.

He drew back, his breathing ragged and uneven as he pressed her back against the pillows. His hands smoothed over her body, following the curve of her breasts, the dip of her waist, the fullness of her hips, and Anna's breath caught when his fingers stopped by the very source of her heat. She couldn't hold back the moan that escaped her when he started to stroke her, slowly, tenderly, until she was almost mindless with desire for him.

'Sam,' she whispered, arching her hips up to meet his tantalising fingers. 'Sam…please!'

They made love with an intensity that moved them both to tears but they were healing tears. As they lay in one another's arms afterwards, their bodies sated, their minds at peace, Anna knew that she had found herself again. The long, difficult months when she had tried so desperately to conceive had robbed her of her womanhood, but now she had regained that part of her, and she had Sam to thank for it. Sam had given her back something precious, something that she hadn't realised had been missing until he had come back into her life. She would be forever in his debt for what he had done.

Day crept in, just a faint lightening of the darkness filtering around the edges of the blind, but Sam was already awake. He'd been awake for hours, dreading the time when morning arrived.

He sighed as he looked at Anna lying beside him. She'd said that she was sure about what they were doing and that she wouldn't regret it, but would she still feel like that when she woke up? He couldn't bear to think that he might have caused her any more anguish, neither could he bear to wonder about the anguish he might have caused himself. Hadn't he sworn that he would keep his distance? So what had he gone and done? Only slept with her, that's what! If that wasn't going to create repercussions for him in the future, he had no idea what would.

He groaned as he tossed back the quilt and got out of the bed. His clothes were in a heap on the floor so he scooped them up and carried them into the bathroom. Stepping into the shower enclosure, he turned the water to the cold setting and let it pound down on his head and shoulders as a penance. OK, so making love to Anna last night had been so wonderful his bones kept turning to liquid whenever he thought about it, but that wasn't the point. He was supposed to be steering clear of any complications, definitely not making new memories to add to his already huge collection.

Five minutes of cold-water torture was all he could stand. A quick blast of hot water and he got out. Helping himself to a towel from the shelf he dried himself off then dressed. He would make some coffee and toast, put it on a tray and take it up to Anna. He certainly wasn't going to slip away without seeing her like some cheap one-night stand. No way! He would face up to what he had done, talk it all through with her if that was what she wanted, behave responsibly…

Responsible? a small voice inside him taunted. Did he even understand the meaning of the word?

'Oh, quieten down!' he muttered, opening the bathroom door and jumping when he suddenly came face to face with Anna. 'Sorry,' he murmured, hastily shifting aside so she could pass him on the tiny landing.

'That's all right.'

She gave him a quick smile but he saw the colour run up her face and knew that she felt awkward about what had happened the night before. If nothing else, at least he could make sure that she had nothing to feel embarrassed about.

He caught her hand and turned her to face him. 'Last night was perfect, Anna. It was what we both needed, too.'

'Are you sure?' She rushed on before he could say anything. 'I thought maybe you were having second thoughts when I realised you'd gone…'

She tailed off and Sam hurriedly stepped in. 'I'm quite sure. I don't regret it, Anna. Not even a tiny bit,' he added as much for his own benefit as hers. 'As for my sudden disappearance, I was about to make some coffee and toast and bring it up to you.'

'Oh, I see.' She gave him a tentative smile. 'That sounds good.'

'Then get yourself back into bed and I'll sort everything out.'

He dropped a kiss on her lips but didn't linger. It seemed wiser not to get too carried away until he was sure about what he was doing. Last night could be explained away as something they'd both needed—however, a second session this morning would be less excusable. Before he made love to Anna again, he had to be one hundred per cent sure about his motives…*if* he made love to Anna again.

The thought of never again experiencing the passion they had enjoyed together was too hard to deal with. Sam chased the prospect from his mind as he ran down the stairs. He filled the coffee-maker then hunted some bread out of the bread-bin and popped it into the state-of-the-art toaster. It took him a couple of seconds to work out the controls and he smiled to himself once he had finally mastered them.

Anna had always loved kitchen gadgets. Unlike many couples where it was the man who bought the latest electrical devices, it had been Anna who had never been able to resist the marketing spiel. Toasters, coffee-makers, the latest mixers—their kitchen cupboards had been packed with her toys. He'd teased her unmercifully about her 'addiction' even though he had encouraged it by buying all the latest equipment for her. He'd loved seeing her face light up as she'd unpacked the latest bit of wizardry.

Opening one of the cupboards, he peered inside but there was no sign of any of the gifts he'd bought for her. Had she got rid of them all after the divorce, as eager to dispense with his presents as she'd been to dispense with the him?

Sam's mouth compressed as he closed the cupboard door and lifted the toast out of the machine. He knew it was stupid to feel hurt about something so inconsequential but he couldn't help seeing it as an indication of her true feelings for him. She'd explained why she had wanted to end their marriage and he understood now why she'd felt that way, even though he didn't agree with her logic. However, that didn't explain why she'd gone to such lengths to expunge him from her life.

He certainly hadn't done that. He still had mementoes of their time together, things he cherished and would never part with, and maybe he should take that as a warning. He mustn't make the mistake of thinking that there might be a place for him in Anna's future.

Once the coffee had been poured, he loaded everything onto a tray and carried it back upstairs. Anna was sitting up in bed and she smiled when he went into the room.

'Room service, too. What a treat.'

'It's the least I could do.' He put the tray on the bedside table and handed her a mug of coffee then sat down on the side of the bed. Picking up the plate of toast, he offered it to her. 'I put strawberry jam on the toast. I hope you still like it for breakfast.'

'I do.' She helped herself to a slice and bit into it, nodding appreciatively. 'You always did make excellent toast,' she murmured with her mouth full.

'Good. At least you have one good memory of our time together,' he said without thinking as he picked up the other mug.

'I have a lot of good memories, as it happens,' she said quietly, putting the slice of toast down on the plate.

'Good,' Sam repeated because he couldn't dredge up enough enthusiasm to think up a different reply.

He took a swig of his coffee and let the fragrant brew trickle down his throat, hoping it would warm away some of the cold uncertainty that filled him. If Anna had really loved him, surely she wouldn't have wanted to get rid of everything to do with him and their marriage?

'What? And before you tell me that everything is fine, I know you, Sam. I can tell when something is bothering you.' She took a quick breath but he heard the strain in her voice. 'Do you regret what happened last night? Is that it?'

'No.' He shrugged. 'Last night was perfect, as I told you. I don't regret it and I don't wish it hadn't happened either.'

'Then what's wrong?' She touched his hand then quickly withdrew her fingers as though she was afraid that she might have overstepped the boundaries in some way. And it was the fact that she could think like that after what they'd shared a few hours before that made him feel even more wretched.

'Why did you get rid of everything that reminded you of our life together?' he asked, knowing that the quickest way to resolve the issue was to be honest with her. 'I checked the kitchen cupboards and you've even got rid of all those gadgets I bought you.'

'There simply wasn't space for all the clutter.' She summoned a smile but he could tell the effort it cost her. 'I had to pare everything down to the barest minimum when I moved here, Sam. That's why I got rid of a lot of unnecessary items. They went to a charity shop so at least they weren't wasted, if that's what's troubling you.'

'It isn't that.' He glanced around the room, taking note of everything in it. There was nothing there he remembered, nothing that came from their former life together. This room, too, had been sanitised, cleared of everything that might remind Anna of their joint past.

He turned to her again, doing his best to keep the pain in check because he didn't want to make a fool of himself. 'It's as though you systematically erased everything to do with me and our marriage from your life, Anna. I bet there isn't even a photograph of us together in this house, is there?'

She flushed at the rebuke in his voice but her gaze didn't waver. 'No. There didn't seem any point hanging onto the past, Sam.'

'Really?' He stood up, unable to sit there while he was forced to face up to the truth. 'You wanted nothing to remind you of how unhappy you'd been—was that it?'

'Yes, if you choose to see it that way.' She sat up straighter, a hint of defiance in her eyes as she stared back at him. 'I wanted to get on with my life, Sam. Is that a crime?'

'No. But most people don't dispense with every single thing after they get divorced. They at least hang onto a few things that remind them of the good times.'

'I didn't want to be reminded about anything, good or bad.' She tossed back the quilt and stood up. 'I'm sorry if you're hurt or offended but I did what I thought was best for me. Now, if you'll excuse me, I need to get ready for work.'

She stalked past him, her head high, her spine rigid, and Sam wished with all his heart that he hadn't said anything. If he hadn't raised the subject, they could have parted as friends if nothing else.

His mind scampered away with the thought of what else he might have had to look forward to before he brought it back in line. There wasn't going to be a fairy-tale ending to this story. There was no chance of him and Anna living happily every after—at least, not together.

He swore softly as he picked up the tray and took it down to the kitchen. Even though he'd known there was no future for them, it still hurt to get a definitive no. He washed up then stowed everything away in its rightful place before heading for the door. At least Anna wouldn't have to cleanse the place after his visit. She could forget all about it and carry on with her life the way she had decided it should be. To all intents and purposes, last night had never happened.

'Everything seems to be settling down again, Helen. The bleeding has stopped and your baby isn't showing any signs of distress.'

Anna looked up from the patient's notes and forced herself to smile. Patients set a lot of store by their physician's expression and the last thing she wanted was for Helen and her husband to think that the prognosis wasn't good because she herself looked unhappy.

'And you're sure the baby will be all right, even though some of the placenta has come away?' Helen asked anxiously.

'Yes. Most of the placenta is still securely attached to your uterus so your baby is receiving everything he needs.' Anna injected a touch more warmth into her voice, hoping it would help to reassure the couple. Just because she was riddled with guilt about the way she and Sam had parted, it didn't mean she should allow her patients to suffer.

'If I was in any doubt about the effect this would have on your baby then I would deliver him early. However, I'm confident that we can and should keep this pregnancy going for as long as possible.'

'Well, if you're sure, Dr Carter, that's good enough

for me.' Helen beamed at her. 'The longer junior stays where he is the better.'

'Exactly. Don't get me wrong, though, Helen. Your baby stands an excellent chance of surviving if I do have to deliver him. However, every extra day he remains in the womb means that he is growing that bit stronger.'

Anna closed the notes and smiled at the couple again, clamping down on the sudden feeling of jealousy that assailed her when she saw how they were holding so tightly to one another. There was no point wishing that *she* had someone to hold onto. As she'd discovered to her cost, sometimes sharing a grief only doubled it.

She blocked that thought from her mind for the simple reason that she couldn't handle it and carried on. 'I'd like to keep a close eye on you for the next few days, Helen. Unfortunately, that means keeping you in over Christmas. I know you'll be disappointed about having to stay here but I do feel it's in yours and the baby's best interests.'

'It doesn't matter,' Helen said firmly. 'So long as this little chap is all right, I'm more than happy to stay, although I don't know how Brian is going to fare. He's never cooked a Christmas dinner before so he's in for a treat!'

Anna laughed when Brian put his head in his hands and groaned. 'I'm sure he'll cope. Anyway, I'll check on you again this afternoon. Just try to rest as much as possible in the meantime.'

Anna left the side room where Helen had been moved and headed to the office. The nursing staff had been decorating the ward and everywhere looked very festive. Although there was no tree, there was lots of tinsel dotted about and a couple of water jugs had been filled with holly. Anna sighed as she looked around. She felt even less like celebrating Christmas after what had happened that morning with Sam.

Wendy was already in the office when Anna arrived. She had the kettle boiling and she smiled when Anna went in. 'That was good timing. Tea or coffee?'

'Tea, please,' Anna replied, sitting down in front of the desk. She ran her hand across the back of her neck. She was developing a tension headache and must try to relax, but the hassle of calling her breakdown service this morning, combined with her complete inability to get Sam out of her head made it virtually impossible. She kept remembering how hurt he had looked when she'd told him that she'd got rid of all the reminders of their life together. At the time it had seemed like the right thing to do but had it been an overreaction? She didn't even have a photograph of them and it seemed wrong all of a sudden that she should have erased such an important part of her life.

'Penny for them.' Wendy placed a mug on the desk and pushed the biscuit tin towards her. 'You look as though the cares of the world have descended on you. What's up, Doc? If you'll pardon the pun.'

'Oh, I'm just tired, I expect.'

Anna dredged up a smile as she reached for a biscuit. Although she liked Wendy, she didn't want to tell her about Sam. She'd told nobody at Dalverston that she was divorced, apart from when she'd filled in her application form for the job and had had to tick the box that had asked about her marital status. As far as every-one in the hospital was concerned she was a single woman, and that's how she intended it to remain.

'It has been hectic lately,' Wendy agreed, reaching for the tin. She groaned when the phone suddenly rang. 'How does this infernal contraption know when I'm about to have a cuppa?'

Anna dutifully laughed as Wendy answered the call. Picking up her mug, she took a sip of the hot tea, won-dering why she felt so unhappy about deceiving every-one. The fact that she and Sam had been married had no bearing on their present positions within the hos-pital. If people found out, it would lead to a lot of gossip and she doubted if Sam would appreciate that any more than she would. However, no matter how hard she tried to reason it all out, it still felt as though she was behav-ing in a very underhand manner.

'Not for me this time, I'm pleased to say.' Wendy hung up and grinned at her. Anna quickly cleared her mind of such unsettling thoughts. She had made her decision and she wasn't going back on it now.

'No? Who was it?'

'ED. They want someone to go down and take a look at a patient. Do you want to do it, Anna, or should I get Pritti to go?'

Anna frowned. 'Pritti's taken an hour off to go to the dentist. She's broken a tooth so I said she could slip out and get it seen to rather than wait until after Christmas. I'm not sure if she's back yet.'

Wendy chuckled as she helped herself to the last

chocolate shortbread. 'Looks like it's your turn, then, Anna.'

Anna sighed as she hauled herself to her feet. 'Who was it who called? Did they give a name?'

'Sam Kearney. Can't say that I know him… Oh, I wonder if he's that new locum who started last week.' Wendy smiled. 'Polly was in raptures about him. To hear her talk, you'd think he was the best thing since sliced bread! You could be in for a treat, Anna.'

Anna turned away so Wendy couldn't see her reaction. The thought of all the women in the hospital lusting after Sam wasn't one she relished. 'I'll ask for him, then. See you later.'

She left the office and headed to the stairs, deeming it quicker to use them rather than wait for the lift. It was just three flights down after all, so not too strenuous. There was no reason in the world why her heart should start racing, none apart from the fact that she was about to see Sam again. After the way they'd parted, she doubted if he would be exactly thrilled to see her.

She sighed as she exited the stairwell and pushed open the door to the ED. Bang went any ideas they'd had about them being friends. After last night, and more especially this morning, there was little chance of that happening.

CHAPTER EIGHT

SAM could feel his insides tying themselves into knots as he waited to see who would respond to his call. Although he hadn't asked specifically for Anna, he knew there was a better than average chance that she would opt to come herself rather than send a junior. His stomach tightened that bit more when he saw the stairwell door open as she arrived. He needed to handle this right, behave in a strictly professional manner. His only concern must be the welfare of his patient, not his own long-dead marriage.

'Thanks for coming so quickly,' he said formally as he went to meet her. He led her to the end cubicle then paused outside while he outlined the patient's case history for her.

'The patient's name is Alison Barker. She's thirty-two and she presented with a range of symptoms including severe abdominal distension, haemodynamic instability and respiratory problems. She's been suffering bouts of nausea and diarrhoea too. I examined her and discovered there's ascites as well.' He shrugged. 'That's probably what is causing the breathing problems. All that fluid is putting pressure on the diaphragm.'

'I see. Obviously, you think it's a gynae problem or you wouldn't have phoned me,' Anna replied quietly.

Sam was relieved to see that she seemed as keen to focus on the patient's problems as he was, and nodded. 'That's right.'

'So, have you any thoughts as to what might be wrong with her?'

'I do, although, to be frank, there could be any number of reasons why this has happened. However, when I read her case notes, I discovered that she'd been a patient here a couple of years ago. Alison and her partner had a whole raft of fertility tests done at the time.'

'And what did the tests show?' Anna asked quietly.

'Nothing conclusive,' he said firmly, because this wasn't the right time to start thinking about all the tests he and Anna had undergone. 'According to Alison's notes, the consultant couldn't find a specific reason why she and her partner couldn't conceive. Once the initial assessment had been done, they were referred to a fertility clinic in Leeds. That was the last we saw of her until today.'

'But you do think there's a link between that and what's happening now?' she clarified.

'Yes. As I say it could be umpteen different things, but the one I keep going back to is OHSS. The symptoms of ovarian hyperstimulation syndrome are almost a perfect match to what the patient has presented with. If it is OHSS, though, we need to know for certain what we're dealing with.'

'Did Alison say if she's been having fertility treatment?'

'No. She clammed up when I asked her. She seems very on edge, scared almost. It's understandable because she's in a lot of pain, but I get the feeling that she is holding something back, which is why I wanted a second opinion. You must have seen cases like this, Anna, so what do you think?'

'From what you've told me, it could very well be OHSS but we need to get the patient to confirm it before we can know that for certain. Have you requested a blood test? Abnormally high levels of oestrogen and progesterone could be a sign that she's been having treatment.'

'The results aren't back from the lab yet,' he explained. 'I know I'm probably jumping the gun, but I didn't want to wait. I have a bad feeling about this case. I'd like to get to the heart of the problem sooner rather than later.'

Anna nodded. 'I agree. If it is OHSS and it's reached such a severe stage, we can't afford to hang around. There's an increased risk of renal failure, not to mention ovarian rupture or even a thrombosis. I'll have a word with her and see if she'll tell me anything.'

'Thanks. I really appreciate it.'

Sam swept the curtain aside and followed her into the cubicle, relieved that he had managed to get through the first stage unscathed. So long as he concentrated on his job, he would manage, he told himself as he went over to the bed. 'Hi, Alison. This is Dr Carter. Actually, I should call her *Miss* Carter because she's a consultant, but I'm sure she won't mind.'

He glanced at Anna, who smiled, trying not to wonder how long it had been after the divorce before she had reverted to her maiden name. One week? Two? He doubted if it had been much longer than that. From what he had gathered that morning, she had been keen to rid herself of any trappings of their marriage.

He breathed deeply as a pain slid, stiletto-like, between his ribs, then carried on. 'Dr Carter is in charge of the obs and gynae unit. I believe you were a patient there a couple of years ago.'

'I...um...that's right,' Alison murmured, her eyes sliding away from his.

Sam frowned when he saw the fear that crossed the young woman's face. He had no idea what she was afraid of but he knew he was right to think that she was hiding something. He glanced at Anna and was relieved when he saw that she had picked up on it as well. Good. At least they wouldn't have to fall back on the old standby of whispering together in the corner while he explained it to her.

His blood heated at the thought of them being en-sconced in such close proximity and he ground his teeth. Down, boy! he told himself sternly, moving aside as Anna approached the bed. She smiled at the other woman, her face showing nothing but concern for Alison's plight, and his spirits instantly deflated. He might be suffering the tortures of the damned but Anna was as cool as the proverbial cucumber around him!

'Hello, Alison. Dr Kearney asked me to have a word with you in case I can help. I believe you have a lot of fluid accumulated in your abdomen and that you've been having problems breathing.'

Alison bit her lip. 'That's right,' she whispered. She closed her eyes, obviously loath to discuss what had caused her present condition.

Sam watched as Anna laid her hand on the other woman's and gently squeezed it. 'There's nothing to get upset about. We just want to help you. Now, according to your notes, you underwent a series of tests to check your fertility levels. Is that right?'

'Yes. They said there was nothing wrong with me or Ben,' Alison muttered.

'So I believe. You were referred to a fertility special-ist in Leeds, weren't you?' Anna continued gently. 'Did they manage to help you?'

Sam felt a lump come to his throat when he realised how poignant it must be for her to ask questions like that. They must be a painful reminder of everything she'd been through and he was suddenly sorry that he had asked for a second opinion, although he knew that he'd had no choice. Maybe he had his suspicions about what might be wrong with Alison but it needed some-one more versed in the subject to confirm it.

'Not really. We had some treatment but it was so ex-pensive. In the end we had to stop.' Tears welled into Alison's eyes and she stopped speaking.

'Fertility treatment is extremely expensive,' Anna said gently. 'And when you need several cycles… Well, there's not many couples who can afford to keep on doing it for ever.'

'Ben was worried in case we got into any more

debt. We'd already taken out a second mortgage on our house and there was no way we could raise any more money.' Alison took a gulping breath. 'I found this place on the Internet, you see. The drugs from there cost only a fraction of what we'd been paying at the clinic. All the doctors kept telling us that there was no physical reason why I couldn't conceive so I thought I'd give it one last go and see if I could conceive naturally.'

'So you sent for these drugs and took them without any proper supervision,' Anna said, struggling to hide her dismay.

'Yes. I used some money my parents had given me for my birthday and saved up the rest by skipping lunch each day. Ben had no idea what I was doing. He was at work when the package arrived and I didn't tell him. Oh, I hated lying to him but I thought it would be worth it if we could just have a baby.'

'Do you know exactly what drugs they were?' Anna pressed her.

'Clomiphene and something else—I can't remember the name now. The company I bought them from told me to take an extra-high dosage so I would be guaranteed to produce more eggs.' Tears were streaming down Alison's face now. 'Ben's off all over Christmas and I thought if I was producing lots of eggs, I'd have a better chance of getting pregnant.'

Sam sighed. It was far worse than he'd imagined and he was only glad that Anna had managed to get at the truth at last. 'I'm glad you've told us the truth, Alison. It means we can help you now that we know what we're dealing with.' He glanced at Anna and raised his brows. 'I'd say it's definitely OHSS, wouldn't you?'

'Yes. I would.' Anna turned to the younger woman. 'You're suffering from ovarian hyperstimulation syndrome, Alison. It's been caused by the high dosage of hormones you've taken to encourage you to ovulate, and the steroids you were probably also given to help any resulting embryos implant themselves in your womb.'

'Ben will go mad when he finds out,' Alison sobbed. 'He said we had to stop and I didn't take any notice of him.'

'I'm sure he'll understand,' Sam said soothingly, wondering how he would have felt if it had been Anna lying there. He shuddered at the thought and hurried on. 'The main thing now is to get you sorted out, and I'm afraid that will mean admitting you to the obs and gynae unit.'

Alison cried all the harder when she heard that but there was nothing else they could do. Sam told the nurse to administer oxygen to assist with her breathing then led the way from the cubicle. There was a tremendous racket going on outside so he escorted Anna to the office where it was a bit quieter.

'Thanks for that, Anna. I doubt I would have got to the root of the problem so quickly if you hadn't been there.'

Anna shrugged. 'I'm sure you would have got the story out of her in the end. It's a real mess, isn't it? To think that people can buy dangerous drugs like that over the Internet and use them without any supervision. Something should be done to stop it.'

'It should,' he agreed, then grimaced. 'I wonder how

many other women have been lured into ordering them by the low prices.'

'I don't know, but I expect there's a lot of people desperate enough to take the chance.'

Her tone was bleak. Sam knew that she was thinking about how desperate they had been at one time, although he would never have allowed Anna to jeopardise her health even if it would have meant them having the child they had craved.

That's where they had differed, though. Anna would have walked over hot coals if it would have meant her having a baby, whereas he would have always weighed up the harm it might cause her. It proved once again how great her need to be a mother had been, and that nothing else could have provided an adequate substitute, not even his love.

His heart ached as the truth was slammed home to him again. It was hard to hide his feelings but he'd got this far and he wasn't about to let the side down. 'Anyway, the damage has been done now, so all we can do is sort things out as best we can.'

'If we can,' Anna said flatly. 'There's no guarantee that Alison won't suffer long-term repercussions from this. I'll see if I can find her a bed, although it might take a bit of juggling. I'll phone you when I've got everything arranged.'

She turned to go but Sam knew he couldn't let her leave without at least attempting to calm the muddy waters that had been stirred up that morning. 'About this morning and what I said, Anna. I had no right to criticise you like that.'

'No, you didn't.' She turned to face him, looking so

cool and in control that if he hadn't known her better, he would have believed that was how she truly felt. However, he could see the tic of a nerve beneath her eye and knew that she was nowhere near as calm as she was pretending to be.

All of a sudden he was filled to the brim with self-loathing. He'd not only criticised the way she had chosen to live her life in the last few years but he'd hurt her as well by his comments. He shook his head in dismay. 'I am *so* sorry. I don't know what got into me. I behaved like a petulant child and you have every right to be annoyed with me.'

'I'm not annoyed, Sam. I'm not anything. I just wish that…' She stopped but he couldn't let her leave it there.

'What? What do you wish?'

'That we had never met. That way neither of us would need to feel sad or sorry or upset, would we?'

'You really mean that?' He couldn't disguise how painful he found it to hear her say that. 'You'd honestly prefer it if we hadn't met?'

'It would have saved an awful lot of heartache, wouldn't it?'

'And meant that we'd have missed out on an awful lot of joy, too, or is that something else you've chosen to erase from your memory?'

His tone was sharp but he wasn't going to apologise for it. Why should he? If she'd run him through with a spear, she couldn't have hurt him any more than she'd done by that revelation.

He spun round on his heel, knowing that he couldn't stand there a moment longer while they dissected the past. Every time they did so it got worse, and if he wasn't careful all his good memories would be completely wiped out, the way Anna had deliberately wiped out all of hers.

'I'll get the paperwork sorted before I send Alison up to you,' he said shortly.

'Fine. I'll let you know when we have a bed ready.'

Anna didn't linger. There was no reason for her to do so. Sam went back to the cubicle and checked the patient's obs again. Anna phoned a short time later to tell him she had a bed ready so he called for a porter. He'd done his bit and now he would hand over Alison into Anna's care. Anna would do everything she could to help the young woman. She was a damned fine doctor and there were few who could match her in his estimation.

That she had felt the same about him at one time was something he had cherished, but maybe he'd been wrong to cling to the thought. Maybe he should shed it along with all the rest, all those pictures he had stored in his mind's eye of the happy times they'd had together.

He'd not needed photographs when he could instantly recall the various events that had led up to their marriage and beyond. Holidays in cottages in the country, meals out in country pubs, hikes over moorland and along seashores: they were all filed away in his internal photo album.

It hadn't mattered that it had invariably rained whenever they'd gone on holiday or had a day out because they had been such good times, times he and Anna had enjoyed together. Nothing could have spoiled those precious days, not even rain, hail or snow. They'd been golden times in his life, times he still cherished. Whenever he was feeling low, in fact, he took out the memories and enjoyed them all over again, but he had to stop doing that from now on. He had to put the past back in its box and turn the key in the lock. It was what Anna had done and it seemed to have worked for her.

Hadn't it?

Sam stopped dead, although it wasn't an old memory that had brought him to a halt but a new one, one from last night, the one in which Anna had told him about her fantasy.

He breathed in deeply, forgot to breathe out, and coughed. If she was free of the past then why had she been fantasising about making love with him? If he was past tense and not present, he shouldn't have figured on her internal Richter scale by so much as a tremor, yet she had told him, quite categorically, that she'd been imagining their love-making from the moment they had met again.

A smile slowly curled his mouth. Maybe Anna wasn't being wholly truthful. Perhaps she didn't envision him being a permanent fixture in her life, but he definitely wasn't a has-been.

Once Alison Barker had been admitted to the ward, Anna set about trying to undo some of the damage. OHSS at this level was a medical emergency and it needed careful management to avoid a tragedy. Strong analgesics were required to ease the pain caused by the abdominal swelling. Anti-emetics were also essential to control the nausea and allow the ingestion of food and fluids. Although vast amounts of fluid were being stored inside the body, more fluids were needed to correct the patient's electrolyte imbalance. Because Alison was unable to pass urine properly, owing to her kidney function being disrupted, she needed to be catheterised. And it went without saying that all fluids, both their intake and their output, needed to be recorded.

Anna ticked off the list of jobs that would need to be done to maintain the patient. Two-hourly checks on her vital signs, a record of her weight as any gain would indicate that more fluid was accumulating in the peritoneal cavity. Alison would also need a complete physical examination twice a day, although care would have to be taken to ensure that no pressure was placed on her swollen ovaries in case they ruptured.

Her circumference was measured around the navel and that would be repeated later that night and again in the morning. An ultrasound examination would be carried out as soon as she was comfortable to check ovarian size and the full extent of the fluid present. A chest X-ray was booked for later in the day and an echocardiogram—essential in case there was any fluid collecting around her heart—was currently under way. That would need to be repeated daily, too.

Then there were twice daily bloods to be taken, serum creatinine levels to be checked and liver enzymes to be monitored. Treatment with diuretics would be considered once an adequate intravascular volume had been restored, but it could take a while to reach that point. As she wrote down exactly what needed to be done, Anna knew that the staff were going to be stretched over the busy Christmas period. They had a lot more patients to attend to and there were only so many hours in a day. It made her see that the tentative plans she'd made to work over the holiday period needed to be firmed up.

'I think that's everything,' she said, glancing at Pritti and her junior registrar, Eamon Riley, who had joined her and Wendy in the office. 'Can you think of anything I've missed?'

Eamon laughed. 'With a list that long, I sincerely doubt it!'

Anna smiled. 'It is a lot to do but it's all essential, I promise you.'

'Oh, I believe you. I'm just glad that I'm off over Christmas and can leave it all to Pritti,' Eamon replied cheerfully.

'Thanks.' Pritti sighed as she scanned the list of instructions. 'What about the drip? I thought you'd have used lactated Ringer's solution.'

'Five per cent dextrose in normal saline is best, given the tendency to hyponatraemia,' Anna assured her. 'Serum concentration of sodium is lower in cases of excessive fluid retention and we need to rectify that.'

'I see.' Pritti made a note on her pad. 'How long will it take to sort this out? I've never dealt with a case like this so I have nothing to compare it to.'

'It's difficult to say. At least a week, maybe longer… Oh, yes, Alison will need full-length venous support stockings to help reduce the risk of a thromboembolism. I've put her down for subcutaneous heparin therapy every twelve hours, haven't I?'

'You have.'

'Then that should cover it for now.' She glanced at Wendy. 'I know it's going to take a lot of extra time so I've decided to work over the Christmas period. An extra pair of hands will be welcome, I imagine.'

'They certainly will, although I do think it's above and beyond the call of duty for you to offer, Anna!' Wendy exclaimed.

Anna shrugged. 'I've nothing better planned so I may as well be here as at home.' She stood up, not wanting to instigate an in-depth discussion about her motives. 'Now I am going home to put my feet up. Have a good one, guys.'

She left the office with a chorus of goodbyes ringing in her ears, although they didn't disguise the fact that her colleagues were obviously surprised by her decision to work over Christmas. However, to her mind it was a great deal better than the alternative. Now she wouldn't have to feel guilty about not buying a turkey and all the trimmings. She could let the festivities pass her by.

She sighed as she headed outside to her car. She had always loved Christmas before the divorce. When she'd been a child, her parents had pulled out all the stops— mince pies and sherry for Santa left on the mantelpiece on Christmas Eve, a bulging stocking hung on the end of her bed for when she'd woken up.

The magic of Christmas had stayed with her even after she'd grown up, and when she and Sam had been first married it had been even more wonderful.

However, in the past three years she had come to dread it. It was hard being on your own when everyone else was celebrating with their families, and she had often felt lonely and left out. At least this year she would have something to occupy her, and that was what she desperately needed at the moment.

Sam had been wrong when he'd accused her of erasing everything to do with their marriage. Oh, she had tried—she'd give him that—but even though she had got rid of all the photographs and the gadgets, she'd never been able to rid her mind of the memories and she never would. Part of her would always hark back to the days when it had felt as though she'd been the luckiest woman alive. She'd had Sam, the man she'd loved, and she'd been almost ridiculously happy. Maybe she should have realised just how much she'd had instead of wishing for the impossible. She and Sam could have been happy once they had got over the disappointment of not having a child.

It was the first time Anna had allowed herself to consider the idea and it scared her. She really couldn't bear to think that she might have made a terrible mistake by letting Sam go.

CHAPTER NINE

CHRISTMAS Eve rolled around and, surprise, surprise, Sam had been rostered to work. He didn't really mind because he had nothing better to do. Although a couple of staff from ED had invited him to various parties over the holiday, he had made his excuses. He didn't feel like celebrating when his life felt so up in the air.

He sighed as he hung his jacket in a locker and reached for his stethoscope. The situation with Anna had really got to him. He found himself thinking about it constantly. It wasn't just the night they had spent together that was on his mind all the time, although it did feature prominently. It was all the rest. How could she wish that they hadn't met? It was incomprehensible to him. Despite all the heartache, he wouldn't ever wish for that to have happened and he found it hard to accept that she felt that way. It was as though she had not only tried to erase their marriage but everything that had made their love so special.

'Looks like someone has a bad case of Christmas Eve blues. Never mind, Sam, you'll soon be back home to see what Santa's brought you.'

'I wish.' Sam dredged up a smile when Jane Burgess, the sister on duty that night, nudged him in the ribs. 'I don't expect Santa's got my address with all the moving around I do.'

'What you need is a good woman to set you on the straight and narrow,' Jane said cheerfully as she followed him out of the staffroom.

'Never mind a good woman. *Any* woman will do,' Ian Roberts, the other registrar working that night, chipped in. 'I don't know about you, Sam, but I'm not the least bit choosy. As long as she isn't throwing up all over me, she'll do. The only women I meet nowadays are always sick!'

Sam laughed. 'Ditto. Maybe we should form a club for hopeless cases like us, Ian.'

'Oh, get away with you!' Jane glared at them. 'All you need to do is make a bit of an effort. There's loads of lovely girls out there, but you two are just too bone idle to go looking for them.'

'That's why I'm pinning my hopes on Santa this year,' Ian retorted, grabbing hold of Jane and whirling her round. 'With a bit of luck, he'll tuck a cuddly little blonde into my stocking who looks just like you... Ouch!' He yelped when Jane clipped smartly him round the ear.

'Less of the cuddly, sonny, if you hope to survive the night,' she threatened him.

Sam chuckled as he left them to it. Everyone seemed to be in remarkably high spirits considering they had such a busy night ahead of them. He went to the desk and picked up the top set of notes from the tray.

'Maxine Jeffries,' he called, looking around the waiting room. Out of the corner of his eye he saw someone walking towards the lifts, and frowned. If he wasn't mistaken, it looked very much like Anna, but surely Anna wouldn't be working on Christmas Eve?

The thought nagged away at him while he worked his way through the list of people waiting to be seen. He dealt with the more serious cases and passed the minor injuries over to the nursing staff. The team at Dalverston was highly trained and they soon cleared the backlog. By ten o'clock the waiting room was empty so Sam decided to take his break.

'I'll go and get something to eat,' he told Jane. 'There's bound to be a rush once the pubs start letting out so I'll take my break now.'

'Fine. I've just sent Angela and Cathy off for their breaks, too,' Jane informed him, referring to a couple of the nurses who were working that night.

'Okey-dokey. Beep me if you need me,' Sam said, heading for the lift. He had just pressed the button when he heard the phone go and he sighed when he realised it was the line that went straight through to the ambulance control centre. Obviously, something was afoot if the control centre had phoned them direct.

The lift arrived but he let it go again, not wanting to leave the department if there was an emergency case on its way in. Jane looked worried when he went back to see what was going on.

'There's been an explosion in the town centre,' she explained. 'The details are very sketchy as yet, but they think a gas main has burst. Ambulance Control has put us on standby to receive the most severely injured.'

'Have they declared a major incident?' Sam asked, frowning.

'Not yet. The emergency services are still assessing the situation.' Jane glanced around the department. 'It's a good job that we managed to get rid of everyone. We'll have a virtually clear run once the casualties start to arrive.'

'Have they any idea of the number we can expect?' He sighed when Jane shook her head. 'In that case, we'll just have to prepare for the worst and see what happens—'

He broke off when the phone rang again. Jane answered it then handed him the receiver. 'They want to speak to the senior doctor on duty.'

Sam took the phone from her. 'Sam Kearney.' He listened intently while the controller explained what they wanted. 'I understand. Yes, I'll get a team together right away.'

He turned to Jane after he'd hung up. 'They want us to send the rapid response unit to the site. It appears the explosion happened in the basement of a nightclub and there are dozens of people trapped in there.'

'Did they say which club?' Jane demanded, going pale. 'My boys have gone into town and I know they were going to one of the clubs…'

'I assume they have mobile phones so go and ring them,' Sam said immediately. He shook his head when she started to protest. 'I'll get everything sorted out here. It's more important that you check on your kids.'

He went to his office after Jane had hurried away and

found the list of staff who worked for the rapid response team. Ian was one of the doctors listed but the other doctor's name was one Sam didn't recognise. He went back out to the desk and checked with Polly, nodding when he discovered that the other man was off sick and that he was acting as his replacement.

'In that case, I'll go in his stead,' he said immediately. He glanced round when Ian appeared along with their senior house officer, Abbey Martin. 'There's been an explosion in one of the nightclubs in town and Ambulance Control wants us to deploy the rapid response team. I'll be going and you are as well, Ian. Abbey, I want you to keep things ticking over in here. It sounds as though there's a lot of casualties and as we're taking the most severely injured, we'll need to draft in reinforcements.'

'I'll get that all sorted out.' Jane had come back now. She nodded when Sam raised his brows. 'They're fine. They were still in the pub when the explosion happened, thankfully.'

'Good.'

Sam didn't waste any more time. As soon as the nurses returned from the canteen, they went to the supplies room and got themselves kitted up. As he zipped up the bright orange flight suit, Sam could feel the adrenaline pumping through his veins. He had no idea what they were going to find when they got to the scene but he would do his best to help the injured. At the end of the day, all anyone could do was his best in any situation.

Had he given his marriage his best shot? he

wondered suddenly. He'd thought he had, but maybe there'd been something more he could have done to save it. As he followed the rest of the team to the ambulances, Sam found himself wishing, rather futilely, that he could turn back the clock and try again. Only this time, he wouldn't let Anna go. *This* time he would move heaven and earth to keep her!

Anna heard about the explosion as she was on her way to check on Alison Baker. A couple of nurses were talking about it when they came back from the canteen. She frowned as she drew back the curtain. It appeared that the rapid response unit had been deployed—had Sam gone with it? She couldn't imagine him staying behind if he thought he could help and it was worrying to imagine him being in danger. It was hard to put aside her fears for his safety as she greeted the young woman.

'Hello, Alison. How are you feeling now? Sister said that you've not been too good tonight.'

'I feel so sick all the time.' Alison groaned. 'And my tummy aches too.'

Anna gently felt her swollen abdomen. 'It's still very distended. If it doesn't settle down in the next couple of hours, I think we shall need to remove the excess fluid from your abdominal cavity.'

Alison gulped. 'Will it hurt?'

'It will be a bit uncomfortable but it shouldn't be too awful for you.' Anna sighed when she saw tears start to trickle down the woman's face. 'Has your husband been in to see you tonight?'

'Yes. He didn't stay very long, though. He's still angry with me because of what I did.'

Alison looked even more miserable and Anna patted her hand. 'He's worried about you and I expect that's why he's annoyed. Plus, the past couple of years must have been a strain for him, too. Undergoing fertility treatment is gruelling. I know that for a fact.'

'Have you been through it?' Alison asked, perking up.

'Yes, I have.' Anna smiled, although she was surprised that she had revealed something so personal to a patient. Would she have done so if Sam hadn't been on her mind all the time? she wondered. Even though she had tried to be sensible, she hadn't been able to stop thinking about him since that night they had spent together. No wonder when it had been the most wonderful night she could remember since way before their divorce.

'I underwent several years of fertility treatment and I know how hard it is on a couple, so be patient with him,' she said, closing her mind to the thought. 'Ben will come round once he gets over his shock.'

She left it at that, not wanting to say any more in case she was tempted to pour out the whole story, and that would be highly unprofessional. She checked Alison's obs then went into the office. There was a stack of paperwork that needed doing and now was as good a time as any. She'd just made a start when the phone rang and she automatically reached for the receiver.

'Obs and Gynae. Anna Carter speaking.'

She listened intently as the operator explained they'd

had a request from the rapid response team. Apparently one of the female casualties trapped by the explosion had gone into labour and the senior doctor on site had requested specialist help.

Anna immediately offered her services and hung up. Wendy was in the ward so she went to find her and explained what had happened then put together a pack of supplies she might need. Within a very short time she was in her car and heading into the town.

The police had set up a cordon around the building but they waved her through when she explained who she was. Parking her car up an alleyway, she ran towards the devastated building, her heart sinking when she saw the damage that had been done to it. Most of the roof had fallen in and part of the front wall was missing, too. Sections were being held up by metal girders put in place by the fire service, but the whole lot looked ready to cave in. It was hard to imagine that anyone had survived the blast but she could see people being ferried out on stretchers.

'Anna! I had no idea you were coming.' All of a sudden Sam was there, his face looking ghostly in the yellow glow of the floodlights that had been set up around the site.

Anna gaped at him. 'Just look at the state of you!'

'It's all the dust in there.' He ran a grimy hand through his hair, setting loose a shower of plaster particles. 'You'll need an overall. There should be a spare one in the back of one of the ambulances. Come on.'

He ushered her to a nearby ambulance and found an overall for her to wear then handed her a hard hat. 'Put that on as well. Although the fire crew have shored everything up, there's odd bits of rubble falling all over the place.'

'What about this patient you want me to see?' Anna demanded, tucking her hair inside the hat and struggling with the strap.

'Here.' Sam quickly fastened it for her then took her arm and guided her towards the building. 'She's definitely in labour but I'm not sure how far along she is because I can't see her properly. She's trapped behind a section of wall and we can't get to her.'

'Is she conscious?' Anna asked, her heart sinking even further.

'No. That's the other problem. We have no way of knowing how far advanced her pregnancy is. The police are trying to find out who she was with but it's a bit chaotic at the moment.'

'Sounds as though we'll have to play it by ear,' Anna said, trying to hide her alarm.

'Yep. But we'll manage.' Sam looped his arm around her shoulders and gave her a hug. He let her go when one of the police officers came over to speak to him.

Anna breathed in deeply to control her racing pulse. It had been a gesture of friendship and nothing more, she told herself firmly as she waited for Sam to finish. By the time he turned to her she had managed to get a grip on herself, although she wasn't sure her composure would last if he hugged her again.

'The police have found some of the women our lady was with. Her name is Lizzie Hutchings and she's twenty-five. It's her first baby and it's due on the second of January.'

'At least it's almost to term,' Anna said thankfully.

'One plus point, eh?'

Sam grinned at her, his teeth gleaming whitely against his grey-coated skin, and Anna found herself immediately responding. It was typical of him to find something good about even the scariest situation.

'Just one. OK, let's take a look at her. If that baby is on his way, I don't want him arriving while his mum's on her own.'

Sam laughed. 'There's no chance of that. There's a whole crew working in there. This little one has his very own reception committee standing by to welcome him into the world!'

Anna chuckled as she followed him into the building. Sam's upbeat attitude was just the antidote she needed. She picked her way across the rubble then paused when they came to what appeared to be a huge hole in the floor.

'This was once the stairwell,' Sam explained. 'The stairs have fallen in so the only way down now is via this ladder. I'll go first and help you. OK?'

'Yes,' Anna said, gulping as she peered into the depths below.

'You'll be fine, Anna. I won't let you fall. Promise.'

Once again he gave her a hug and once again her pulse went into overdrive, but she didn't bother searching for a reason for him hugging her this time. Quite frankly, she didn't care when it felt so good!

'Right, you can come on down. I'll guide your foot onto the first rung and it will be a snip after that.'

Anna knelt down and eased her right foot over the

edge of the hole, floundering a little as she searched for the ladder.

'Here you go.' Sam grasped her ankle and guided her foot onto the rung then helped her find the next one until she had got the measure of them. He caught hold of her arm and helped her onto the floor when she reached the bottom. 'See. That wasn't too bad, was it?'

'No, it was fine.' She smiled back at him, seeing the concern in his eyes. Had he been worried in case she'd been frightened during the descent? she wondered, and knew it was true. Reaching up she touched him lightly on the cheek. 'Thanks, Sam. I appreciate you taking such good care of me.'

'It's all I ever wanted to do,' he said softly, and she knew that he wasn't referring to the current situation.

A lump came to her throat and she had to swallow before she could reply. 'I know.'

'I hope so.'

He didn't say anything else but he didn't need to because Anna understood. He didn't want to push her, didn't want to make things difficult for her in any way. Sam had always put her first and he always would. It was what had made her fall in love with him in the first place. At some point in the past she had forgotten that and it was a shock to rediscover it, but a pleasant one.

As she followed him across the basement, Anna promised herself that she wouldn't forget it again. She would make a point of remembering how much Sam had always cared about her and enjoy the feelings it aroused inside her. It was one very special and very precious memory she didn't intend to lose ever again.

CHAPTER TEN

'I'LL see if I can organise some more light over here. Hold on a second. I won't be long.'

Sam stood up and made his way across the cellar. There was a crew working on a section of the ceiling and he managed to persuade them to lend him one of their high-powered lamps. Anna hadn't moved when he got back. She was still crouched against the section of wall that hid Lizzie Hutchings from view. She looked up when he appeared and he saw the concern on her face.

'Her contractions are becoming more frequent. I've managed to squeeze my hand through the gap and I can feel them. How long before they can get her out of here?'

'They can't remove that wall until they're sure the upper floor has been secured,' Sam explained, crouching beside her. He switched on the lamp and aimed its beam through the narrow gap they'd managed to make in the bricks. 'Is that any better?'

'Let me see.'

Anna lay flat on her stomach and peered through the

gap. Sam felt a wave of tenderness well up inside him when he realised that she looked almost as filthy as he did. There was muck and plaster dust in her hair and smears of dirt all over her once pristine overalls.

'I can see her now. If I can just remove this brick…' She eased a brick out of the way and a second. 'Brilliant! I think I can just about squeeze through that gap now.'

'No way.' Sam put his hand on her shoulder. He shook his head when she looked at him in surprise. 'It's far too risky, Anna. If that wall collapses, you'll be trapped as well. I won't let you take such a risk.'

'And if I don't take it, that baby will have to deliver himself.' She sat up and stared at him. 'It's not much of a choice, Sam, is it?'

'If anyone is going to squeeze through there it's going to be me,' he said firmly.

'Really?' Anna raised her brows. 'Go ahead, if you think you can fit.'

Sam ground his teeth. They both knew there was no way that he would be able to squeeze through such a narrow opening. Anna sighed softly.

'I know it's risky but there really isn't any choice. Someone has to deliver that baby and I'm the best person for the job.'

'All right, but only if the crew says it's safe. Promise me that you'll abide by their decision.'

'Cross my heart,' Anna replied, matching her actions to her words.

Sam chuckled as he got to his feet again. 'Anyone looking at you would think that butter wouldn't melt in your mouth but you don't fool me, Anna Kearney. You stay exactly where you are while I get one of the guys over here.'

He went to find the office in charge and explained what they were proposing. It was only as he led the man back to where Anna was waiting that he realised what he'd said. She was no longer Anna Kearney, of course, yet the name had tripped so naturally off his tongue that he'd not given it a moment's thought. He shot a wary glance at her but he couldn't tell if she'd noticed his gaffe or not. Hopefully, she'd been too concerned about their present dilemma to worry about it.

In the end it was agreed that Anna could make her way through to the other side of the wall. Sam held his breath as he watched her inch her way between the crumbling bricks. Bending down, he opened the bag of supplies, trying to rid his mind of the danger she was in and focus on what needed to be done first.

'Tell me what you want and I'll pass it through to you.'

'The antiseptic wipes, some gloves and a couple of drapes,' she listed. 'Oh, and a stethoscope if you've got one handy.'

Sam sorted through the pack and handed her everything she'd requested. 'Is that it?'

'For now, yes…' She broke off and his stomach muscles bunched at the sudden silence that ensued.

'Anna? What's happening?'

'Another contraction's just started. I want to time the intervals between them so hang on.'

Once again there was silence while Sam mentally

chewed his nails. It was a relief when he heard her voice again. 'Roughly two minutes apart and she's almost fully dilated. Can you pass that light through? I need to see what's going on.'

Sam passed the lamp through the gap which meant he was left in semi-darkness, and that seemed to raise his anxiety levels even more. He was very much aware that Anna was on one side of the wall and he was on the other. He would be powerless to help her if anything happened.

'What can you see?' he demanded, needing the vocal contact more than ever now.

'The baby's head has crowned so it won't be long now… Ah, here we go.'

There was another lengthy pause. Sam lay down and flattened himself against the rubble, ignoring the discomfort caused by chunks of brick digging into his flesh. He needed to see Anna and make sure she was all right. By twisting his head awkwardly to the side, he could just see her, kneeling beside the other woman. She must have sensed he was watching her because she glanced over her shoulder and grinned at him.

'I'm fine. Don't be such an old worry-wart.'

'Can I help it if I'm made like this?' Sam retorted with more than a touch of asperity, and she chuckled.

'No. And I wouldn't have you any other way either.'

Sam felt his emotions see-saw and it was a scary feeling when he needed to be in control of himself. He hastily cleared his throat. 'How long do you reckon it will be before the baby arrives?'

'Not very long, from the look of things.'

Anna was all business again as she spread a green drape on the floor beneath the young mum's hips. Maybe she regretted what she'd said, or maybe it hadn't meant anything to her. At any other time Sam would have chewed it over and tried to extract the truth, but he simply didn't have the time. He glanced round when one of the fire crew tapped him on the shoulder, his stomach sinking when he saw the expression on the other man's face.

'What's wrong?' he demanded.

'We've found another casualty.' The man gestured to the opposite side of the cellar, which had suffered some of the worst damage. 'I don't think there's much hope, Doc, but if you could take a look, please?'

'Of course.' Sam bent down and called through the opening. 'I have to go and check on someone else. I'll be as quick as I can, Anna.'

He heard her murmur something but he was on his feet by then and didn't catch what she said. He followed the fireman to the corner and crouched down beside the body of a young man. There was blood on his forehead and his face was ashen, his lips blue-tinged from lack of oxygen. Sam didn't hold out much hope but he placed his fingers on the carotid artery and jumped when he discovered there was a pulse, albeit a very faint one.

'He's alive,' he said, glancing up. 'Get a stretcher down here, stat! And tell the paramedics I need some fluids.'

Sam didn't waste any time checking that his instructions were being carried out. He quickly examined the young man, nodding to himself when he listened to his chest. There was no sign of air entering the right lung, which could mean that it had collapsed, and that would explain the problems the fellow was having breathing. Now all he needed to do was ascertain why the lung had deflated.

The answer was easily found: a couple of ribs had been broken. Sam would have laid good money on the fact that one of the ribs had punctured the pleura, the membrane lining the chest cavity. Blood had then accumulated in the pleural cavity, forcing the lung to collapse, and now he would need to drain it away and relieve the pressure.

'Fetch me my pack, would you?' he instructed, ripping open the young man's shirt. He nodded his thanks when one of the crew handed it to him. Rooting through it, he found what he needed and set to work, cleaning a section of skin a few inches below the man's right armpit with an antiseptic wipe. Next he took a scalpel and sliced through the flesh, grunting as he cut deeper and hit the tough intercostal muscle, which joined the ribs together. After widening the opening with the tip of a freshly gloved finger, he inserted a narrow plastic tube into the hole and attached it to a drainage bottle. Blood immediately began to gush out of the chest cavity and collect in the bottle.

'A simple haemothorax,' Sam announced, glancing up. He checked the patient's pulse and nodded in satisfaction. 'That's better. It works wonders when you can get some oxygen into your lungs.'

By the time the paramedics arrived with a stretcher,

the patient was starting to come round. Sam quickly re-assured him then handed him over to the ambulance crew. His job there was done and he needed to get back to Anna.

He picked his way across the cellar and took up his previous position on the floor. Anna had her back to him but at least he had visual contact and that was something to be grateful for. 'How's it going?' he called, hoping she couldn't hear the emotion in his voice. This was starting to get silly. He'd only been away from her for ten minutes and he couldn't possibly have missed her!

'Good. The shoulders are clear now... Oh, here we go again.'

She leant forward, giving him a perfect view of her shapely backside, and Sam bit back a groan. He blinked a couple of times to clear the images that had formed in his mind's eye before he looked again, and smiled when he saw that she was holding the baby in her hands. As Sam watched, she turned the infant over and gently patted its back, smiling when it let out an almighty scream of protest.

'It's a little boy and he's gorgeous!' she announced happily.

Sam felt his eyes mist when he saw the delight on her face. 'That's great, Anna. Really great.' He rolled over, raising his voice so he could make himself heard above the din. 'It's a boy, guys!'

A huge cheer erupted at the news. Sam turned back onto his stomach and watched as Anna cut the cord then tenderly wrapped the infant in a sterile drape. She gave him a quick cuddle then handed him through the gap to Sam.

'Take good care of him,' she said, her fingers clinging to the end of the drape for a moment before she reluctantly let go.

'I shall,' he promised, and meant it with every scrap of his being. He might not have been able to help Anna make her dreams of motherhood come true but at least some other woman was going to have a lifetime of happiness ahead of her.

Those wretched tears welled up again and he scrambled to his feet before he made a complete fool of himself. He wouldn't normally describe himself as an emotional person, but it was different when he was with Anna—he reacted very differently around her.

'I'm going to take him out to the ambulance while you attend to Mum,' he shouted. 'I'll be as quick as I can.'

'Just be careful climbing up that ladder,' she instructed anxiously and his aching heart ached that bit more. As he picked his way across the rubble with the babe snuggled securely in his arms, Sam could imagine her saying the same thing to her own children. How unfair it was that she would never be able to shower all that love on a child she had borne.

Holding the infant in one arm, he carefully climbed the ladder and made his way outside, blinking when he was greeted by what seemed like dozens of dazzling bright flashes. It appeared the press had arrived and that he and the baby were ideal front-page fodder.

Ignoring the shouts from the waiting journalists who

wanted a story to accompany their photographs, Sam made his way to the nearest ambulance and handed over the infant, making sure the crew knew that he should be taken to Dalverston General to await his mother's arrival. He was on his way back to the building when there was an almighty roar as another section of the ground floor caved in.

'Anna!' Sam could feel his blood pounding in his veins as he raced towards the building. There were clouds of dust billowing out from it, making it impossible to see clearly, but he struggled on. It was only when one of the fire crew grabbed hold of him that he was forced to stop.

'Anna's in there!' he yelled at the man. 'We've got to get her out!'

'We will, Doc, but we need to assess the situation first. If you go rushing in there, the rest of the floor could collapse as well.'

Sam understood the sense of that. However, it didn't ease the fear that was turning his blood to ice. He hurried over to the section leader. 'How many people are still down in the basement?'

'Six of our crew plus that lady doctor and the woman who's just had that baby,' the man replied, grim-faced.

Sam's heart hit ground level. That meant there were eight people in the cellar who would need rescuing. Although he knew the team would do their best to get them out, Anna and Lizzie Harding were at the far side of the cellar and it could take hours before the crew reached them.

'I need to get down there.' He shook his head when

the older man started to protest. 'There are people injured in there so there's no point telling me I can't go in.'

'Fair enough, Doc, but you'll have to hang fire while we see how safe it is. We can't have you rushing around in there and causing another catastrophe.'

Sam conceded the point with bad grace, but it felt as though a lifetime had passed before the crew decided it was safe for him to descend into what remained of the cellar. As he looked around at the heaps of rubble, Sam experienced a fear unlike anything he had known before. Somewhere under all this mess was Anna, but was she alive?

It was a question he couldn't answer but he knew that if Anna had died, he may as well have died with her. His life would have no meaning if Anna was no longer around and if, by the grace of God, she had survived, then he intended to tell her that.

Anna had just finished delivering the placenta when she heard an almighty roar. It was instinct that made her throw herself across her patient and it was that which saved her own life. She gasped as she saw a section of the wall teeter and fall into the space where she'd been sitting.

Wiping the choking dust off her face, she sat up and tried to get her bearings, but the lamp had been broken. All she was left with was her penlight and its beam was barely enough to pierce the darkness.

'First things first,' she muttered, checking that Lizzie hadn't been hit by any of the debris. Amazingly, the girl appeared to be unharmed so that was a bonus. However, when Anna explored further she realised their situation was dire. From what she could tell, she and Lizzie had been entombed by the falling bricks, and it was scary to sit there in the darkness and wonder if anyone knew they were there.

'Don't be stupid!' Anna told herself out loud. Of course people knew they were there. Apart from the crew who'd been working in the cellar, Sam knew, and he would definitely make sure someone got them out.

She checked the girl's pulse, not needing light to do that as she could assess it by instinct after all these years. It was within an acceptable range and Lizzie's breathing was steady, too. She switched on the torch and sighed when she saw the blood pooling on the ground under the girl's hips. Bleeding after a birth was quite normal, but this was heavier than she would have liked it to be. In the hospital she would have had Lizzie on a drip but there was no chance of that here, so she would have to monitor her very closely.

'Anna! *Anna!* Can you here me?'

The sound of Sam's voice calling her name made her jump. Scooting round on her bottom to where she imagined the opening had been, she shouted back. 'I'm here, Sam. Can you hear me?'

'Yes! Loud and clear, sweetheart.'

His voice sounded louder now and Anna felt tears well in her eyes. Just knowing he was there made her feel so much better. She pressed her hands against the bricks that separated them, wishing she could touch him.

'How long will it take them to get us out?' she asked, struggling not to cry.

'I'm not sure, darling, but they'll be as quick as they can. Are either of you hurt?'

'No, but Lizzie's bleeding quite heavily. She needs to be put on a drip as soon as possible.'

'I'll make sure everything is ready for when we get you out. You just hang in there. It won't be long. Promise.'

Anna gave a shaky little laugh. 'So you perform miracles as well, do you, Dr Kearney?'

'Only when the situation warrants it,' he replied, his deep voice holding a hint of laughter.

'Well, if the current situation meets your criteria, would you mind miracling up a nice big glass of brandy for me? I could do with something to steady my nerves.'

'No problem. One large and very expensive glass of brandy will be ready and waiting for you. Anything else?'

'Hmm, something to eat. I'm starving!'

'What would madam like? After all, we're talking miracles here so anything is possible. Freshly caught Arctic salmon, lobster thermidor, some of those really expensive mushroom thingies which you love and taste like slivers of day-old socks to me.'

Anna chuckled. 'You mean truffles.'

'That's it. I think they should let the pigs have them. After all, they do all the work to find them so why shouldn't they enjoy the rewards?'

'Dream on!' Anna hooted. 'Do you have any idea how much that stuff costs per ounce?'

'No, and I don't want to know either. I'm sure the money could be spent on something a lot more useful.'

'I thought you just offered to get me some,' she pointed out, amazed that they were having such a crazy conversation in such dire circumstances.

'If it's what your heart desires, Anna, I shall stop at nothing to get them for you,' he assured her, and she laughed again.

'I might just hold you to that! Be warned.'

'You can hold me to anything you want and I won't mind,' he said and she shivered when she heard the emotion in his voice.

Bending down, she checked on Lizzie again, using the few seconds it took to gather her composure around her. It was because she felt so vulnerable by being trapped there in the dark that was making her think such foolish thoughts, she told herself. There was no chance of her and Sam getting back together—no chance at all!

CHAPTER ELEVEN

IT WAS the longest night of Sam's entire life. As the hours passed and there was still no sign of Anna being freed, he felt as though he must have aged a hundred years. Every time he had to leave her to attend to another casualty who had been dug out of the rubble, he suffered the tortures of the damned. What if the wall caved in while he was away from her? What would he do then?

The questions ran in an endless loop around his head until he thought he would go mad. Oh, he understood what the fire crew were telling him, that they couldn't just dig, willy-nilly, in case the rest of the ceiling fell in. However, understanding the logistics of the operation didn't help his shattered nerves. By the time the decision was made to start clearing away the bricks that were entombing the two women, he was a wreck.

He stood to one side, desperately wanting to help yet terrified that he would get in the way if he did. The best he could do was act as labourer and pile up the rubble as it was removed. A small gap slowly appeared and then there was another delay while the crew assessed the situation again. Sam tried to curb his frustration for Anna's sake. If it was nerve-racking for him, how bad must if be for her?

'We're nearly there, Anna,' he shouted. 'Another couple of minutes and you'll be out.'

'Make sure you have that brandy waiting,' she shouted back, and everyone laughed.

Sam felt incredibly proud of her then. Most people would have had hysterics if they'd found themselves in this situation but she was behaving with typical fortitude. When the last section of rubble was finally removed, he hurried forward. Kneeling down, he held out his hand and gripped tight hold of hers.

'Come on, sweetheart. Out you come.'

She scrambled through the gap, straight into his arms. Sam hugged her for a moment then forced himself to let her go because if he didn't do so then he might never find the strength to release her. He turned to the section leader.

'I'll check on our patient. Can you pass that stretcher through once I'm inside?'

He crawled through the opening and knelt beside Lizzie. A quick check of her pulse and breathing soon reassured him that she was well enough to be moved, not that there was any danger of them leaving her there. Getting the stretcher out of the cellar wasn't easy but the crew were experts at such operations. Nevertheless, by the time they reached the ambulance Sam was exhausted and he could tell that Anna felt the same.

'You go back in the ambulance with Lizzie,' he instructed once the girl had been loaded on board.

'What about my car?' Anna protested.

'Leave it here.' He put his hands on her shoulders and gently squeezed them. 'You're in no fit state to drive, Anna, are you?'

'Not really, no.' She let her head fall forward onto his chest and he heard her take a deep breath. 'It's been one heck of a night, Sam, hasn't it?'

'It has indeed,' he said thickly. He pulled her into his arms and held her close for a moment but, mindful of the watching journalists, didn't kiss her as he longed to do. He would have to save that pleasure for later—if she would let him.

A tiny fear started to rear its ugly head but he stamped it down. He simply couldn't deal with anything else at the moment. He gave her another quick hug then helped her into the ambulance. 'Off you go. I'll catch up with you later.'

'You're not going back inside that building, are you, Sam?' she said hurriedly as the paramedics started to close the doors.

'No. Everyone's out now. I just need to check on the rest of my team and then we'll be heading back to the hospital.'

'Oh, right.'

She gave him a quick smile before the doors closed, but it was more than enough for Sam. It felt as though he was floating several inches above the ground as he went to find his teammates. Anna may not have said as much in so many words, but she cared about him. It had been obvious from the way she had looked at him just now and the thought made him want to turn cartwheels for joy. Maybe, just maybe, there was some hope left for them after all.

It was almost six a.m. by the time Anna got home and she was frozen. Having left her car in town, she'd had to walk all the way because there were no buses on Christmas Day. She turned up the heating as soon as she got in and put some coffee on then hurried upstairs. A hot shower should help to warm her up.

Ten minutes later she was sitting by the fire, wrapped in her dressing-gown and sipping a mug of steaming coffee. Although it had been a long night, she felt too keyed up to sleep and had decided to sit downstairs for a while. She was just wondering if she should risk a second cup of coffee when she heard a knock on the front door.

Her heart was thumping as she got up to answer it because she knew who it would be. There was only one person it could be at this hour of the day. Her hands were trembling as she opened the door and saw Sam standing on the step. She knew that she had given herself away by letting him see how concerned she'd been about him, and wasn't sure what was going to happen now. It all depended on what she wanted, pre-sumably, and she wasn't sure about that either.

Did she want Sam back in her life? A couple of weeks ago she would have denied it, but she was no longer certain of anything any more. Being with him again had shown her how much she had missed him. It had also shown her how much she still loved him.

However, she couldn't just discount the issues that had led to the break down of their marriage either.

'Hi! I'm glad you're still up.' He held up a plastic carrier bag and grinned at her. 'I come bearing gifts so can I come in?'

'Of course.' Anna led the way into the sitting room, doing her best to behave as naturally as possible. 'Would you like a cup of coffee? It is fresh.'

'I'd love one.' Sam folded his long frame into a chair and sighed. 'I don't know about you, but I'm pooped.'

'Me, too,' she admitted, walking into the kitchen to pour the coffee. She placed the mug on the table beside him then sat down on the sofa. She knew that she needed time to work out what she wanted to do so she decided to steer the conversation round to more general topics. She definitely didn't want to rush into a situation either of them would come to regret. 'How did your team get on? They made it back safely, I hope.'

'Yes, they did, I'm glad to say. What about Lizzie Hutchings?' he asked, taking his cue from her.

'She's fine. She'd had a bump on the head, which was why she'd passed out, but it was nothing major,' Anna assured him. 'The neurosurgical reg ordered a CT scan but nothing showed up. We'll keep her under observation for the next forty-eight hours but it's purely a precaution.'

'That's great,' Sam said sincerely. 'And how about our little chap? Is he doing OK, too?'

'Oh, yes. The last I saw of him he was fast asleep, oblivious to all the fuss that greeted his arrival.' Anna smiled, unable to hide her delight at the baby's safe arrival, and heard Sam sigh.

'You did a superb job of delivering him under the most difficult circumstances, Anna. It's thanks to you that both Mum and child came through their ordeal safely.'

'I only did my job,' she said lightly, although she was touched by his praise.

'Maybe you see it as that, but if it weren't for your bravery in going down into that cellar, the outcome might not have been anywhere near as favourable.'

'You'll make me blush if you say things like that,' she admonished him. 'Anyway, I wasn't the only one in that basement, don't forget. You were there too, Sam, so you should take a lot of the credit.'

'Thank you.' He smiled as he raised his mug aloft. 'How about a toast to us and a job well done, then?'

'I'll drink to that.' She chinked her mug against his then put it back on the table. They seemed to have exhausted that topic and it was time to move on. 'So now that we've finished congratulating ourselves, what was that you said about presents when you arrived?'

Sam chuckled as he picked up the carrier bag. 'Remember when we were in the basement and you told me all the things you fancied?'

'Y-es,' she replied cautiously.

'Well, I didn't manage to find exactly what you requested. There was only one shop open and the stock was rather limited, but I did my best.' He dipped into the bag and pulled out a miniature bottle of brandy. 'Not quite the expensive liquor I promised you but it should be drinkable.'

Anna laughed as she took it from him. 'Thank you very much.'

'There's more to come.' He put his hand back into the bag and pulled out a plastic-wrapped tray of pâté next. 'This *claims* to have genuine truffles in it, although I can't guarantee it.'

Anna shook her head as she added it to the brandy. 'The fact that you found it in the first place amazes me.' She frowned as he started poking around in the bag again. 'Hang on. I don't remember asking you for anything else.'

'You didn't, but it seemed a bit mean to arrive with just a couple of paltry gifts.' He began stacking items on the table. 'There's a tin of lobster, a packet of smoked salmon, some of that Italian bread you like so much—ciabatta, I think it's called. A piece of Stilton cheese and some grapes to go with it. A bottle of wine and…oh, yes, some chocolates, too.'

'I don't know what to say.' Anna stared at the goods in astonishment. 'I also don't know what I'm going to do with all this food!'

'The first bit's easy. You just say "Thank you, Sam."' He paused expectantly.

'I…um…thank you, Sam,' Anna repeated dutifully.

'It's my pleasure.' He smiled at her although she could tell that he was weighing up his next words with care. She felt her heart turn over because all of a sudden she knew what was coming.

'The next bit isn't quite as easy so take your time

before you answer, Anna. Whatever you say, though, I shall abide by your decision.'

Anna wetted her parched lips. 'And what exactly do I have to decide?'

'Whether or not we can share this food.' He looked deep into her eyes and she shivered when she saw the urgency in his gaze. 'I can't think of anything I want more than to spend this Christmas Day with you, Anna, if you'll let me.'

Sam could feel his heart pounding like a jackhammer. The noise it was making was so loud that it drowned out everything else. He saw Anna's lips move, although he couldn't hear the actual words she was saying. He had to ask her to repeat them and cursed himself for piling on the agony.

'Sorry. Can you say that again? I didn't catch it.'

She gave him an odd look. 'I asked you if you thought it was wise for us to spend the day together.'

'If you want the truthful answer, I have no idea.' He leant forward, praying that he could convince her to go along with his plan. All right, so he still had doubts, but the negatives were far outweighed by the positives in his opinion. He cleared his throat, determined to put forward as strong a case as possible.

'I can't put my hand on my heart and swear that we won't be making a mistake, Anna. I just know that I want to spend today with you.'

'Why? What's the point, Sam? We had our chance and it didn't work.'

'I know that.' He captured her hands and held them

tightly in his. 'But there's nothing to say that we can't make it work this time, is there?'

She was shaking her head before he had finished speaking. 'No. The situation is exactly the same as it was before. I still can't give you a child, Sam.'

'I understand that, but having a child wasn't the only thing I ever wanted from you, Anna.' He pulled her towards him and kissed her softly on the mouth. 'I wanted you for yourself, for the beautiful, special person you are. A child would have been the most wonderful bonus, my darling, but not having one didn't make me love you any less.'

'I want to believe you, Sam, but I know how important family is to you.' She tried to pull her hands away but he refused to release her.

'And I'm not denying it, Anna. In an ideal world we would have had a couple of kids and raised them together, but sometimes life doesn't work out the way you imagined it would. You have to adapt to what you can have and live with it.'

'And you honestly believe you can do that? You can swear that five or even ten years down the line you won't feel cheated?'

'Yes, I can!' he replied hotly, and kissed her again. Obviously, he wasn't making much headway trying to convince her with words so perhaps he would have more success this way, he reasoned.

Her lips clung to his for a moment before she pushed him away. 'No. This is too important to be settled by sex. We're talking about our future here and I, for one, am not sure if I can go through a repeat of what we went through before.'

'But it won't be anything like it was before! We know that we can never have a child and that's it. There will be no more punishing fertility treatment, no more having our hopes raised only to have them dashed. We will settle for what we have, Anna, and to my mind that is something far too precious to give up on.'

'I don't know…. You make it sound so simple, Sam, but life isn't like that.'

'That's where you're wrong, sweetheart. It is simple—if you love me as much as I love you.'

Sam held his breath. He knew he was taking a huge risk by blurting out his feelings but he had no choice. If he didn't manage to convince Anna that they could be happy together, he wouldn't get another chance. The thought made him go cold.

'You love me?' she whispered, staring at him with eyes that were filled with wonderment.

'Yes. I never stopped loving you, Anna. Oh, I tried, believe me, but you're part of me. It's no more possible for me to stop loving you than it is to stop breathing.' He captured her hands and raised them to his lips. 'The past three years have been hell. I've spent them wandering about because if I stopped moving I had to think, and that was the last thing I wanted to do. Losing you, Anna, was like losing myself.'

Tears ran down her cheeks as she withdrew her hands and cupped his cheeks. 'I never meant to hurt you, Sam. I was trying to protect you.'

'I know.' He smiled at her even though he could feel

tears threatening him, too. 'That's why I agreed when you asked me for a divorce. I wanted to save you from any more pain when you'd been through so much already.'

'I always wanted a family,' she said wistfully.

'I know, sweetheart,' he said, his heart aching when he saw the sadness on her face. Just for a moment he found himself wondering if it was right to ask her to come back to him when it would be a constant reminder of her shattered dreams. However, the alternative didn't bear thinking about. He didn't think he could live out the rest of his life without her.

The thought tipped him over the edge and he reached for her. Her body felt soft and pliant in his arms as he rained kisses over her face. She didn't resist, although she didn't respond either. Sam knew that she still wasn't sure, and that he had his work cut out to convince her, but they could make this work. He was sure about that!

He kissed her hungrily on the mouth, his heart lurching when he felt her suddenly kiss him back. When she wound her arms around his neck, he could have shouted for joy if his lips hadn't had more important matters to attend to. He went down on his knees in front of the sofa, cradling her against him as he kissed her with increasing urgency, and Anna was with him every step of the way. When he reached for the belt on her robe, she undid it for him, shrugging the bulky towelling off her shoulders. All she had on was a pair of red satin pyjamas and he groaned.

'Do you have any idea how delectable you look?'

'No,' she whispered, smiling at him. 'Maybe you'd better show me.'

She lay back against the cushions and held out her arms. Sam wasted a second pulling his sweater over his head then another one trying to undo his shirt. In the end he dragged it off, still fastened, and grimaced when he heard a couple of the buttons rip off.

Anna laughed. 'Why do I get the idea that you're in a bit of a hurry?'

'I don't know.' He grinned lasciviously at her as he tossed the shirt onto the floor. 'Could it be because I can't wait to unwrap my Christmas present?'

Anna chuckled. 'So what's stopping you?'

'Nothing…absolutely nothing at all,' he growled, his hands reaching for the buttons down the front of her pyjama top.

They made love right there in the living room with the soft grey light filtering through the window. Sam knew that he would remember how Anna looked that day until he died. Maybe there were issues that still needed to be resolved, and maybe it wouldn't be plain sailing from here on, but this day marked a turning point in his life—it had given him back hope for the future, a future he wanted to spend with Anna. It was the best Christmas present he'd ever had!

CHAPTER TWELVE

ANNA put the finishing touches to the table then stepped back to admire her handiwork. Bearing in mind that she hadn't been planning on celebrating Christmas this year, she was rather pleased with what she'd achieved. She had laid the table with her best china and glassware, hunting out some bright red linen napkins which one of her patients had given her as a thank-you gift a couple of years before. She'd even managed to find some greenery in the tiny back garden and had arranged it around a chunky vanilla-scented candle to make a suitably festive centrepiece.

'Mmm, something smells good. It looks good, too. You *have* been busy.'

She shivered when Sam came up behind her and drew her back against him so he could kiss the nape of her neck. After making love in the sitting room they had gone upstairs to her bedroom and made love again in there. Anna wouldn't have believed it was possible to experience the depth of emotion that she'd felt in Sam's arms. It wasn't just the physical satisfaction of making love with him, but how in tune she felt with him mentally as well. He was her soul-mate and being back with him again had shown her just how empty her life had been without him.

The depth of her feelings scared her a little because everything was still so new. She smiled up at him, knowing that she had to hold a bit of herself back until she was sure about what they were doing. Although Sam claimed he could be happy without them having children, she couldn't quite rid herself of the old fears. The last thing she wanted was for him to regret his decision.

'Thank you kindly. We have truffle pâté to start followed by lobster thermidor. No turkey, I'm afraid. Santa forgot to deliver it.'

'Naughty old Santa,' Sam growled, nibbling the side of her neck and smiling wolfishly when he felt her tremble.

'Naughty Santa indeed,' she agreed tartly. She went to step back but Sam held onto her. His expression was sober when he turned her to face him.

'You're sure you're all right about this, Anna? I haven't rushed you?'

'Yes, you have,' she replied truthfully, then smiled. 'But I probably needed rushing, Sam. If I'd had time to think then I might not have made the right decision.'

'So long as you think it's the right one...'

'It is.' She stopped him before any more doubts could creep in. There would be time enough for them later, no doubt, but for now she wanted to enjoy what they had. She gestured towards the bottle of wine. 'If you could open that, I'll check on the lobster.'

Sam didn't pursue the subject. Maybe he felt the

same as she did and wanted to enjoy the day and not spoil it by worrying about what the future might bring.

The lobster was almost ready. Although the meat had come out a tin, Anna had made a rich cheese sauce flavoured with white wine, mustard and shallots, and arranged it all in a pretty gratin dish. The pâté was already arranged on plates with some salad leaves which she'd happened to have in the fridge so in a very short time they were ready to eat.

'That was delicious,' Sam declared some time later, scraping the last trace of sauce off his plate. 'My compliments to the chef.'

'Thank you kindly.' Anna gathered up the dishes and stacked them in the dishwasher. 'It isn't over yet, though. There's still chocolates and brandy to come.'

'Now you really are spoiling me.' Sam put his arm round her waist as she came back to the table and pulled her down onto his lap. He kissed her on the mouth then drew back. 'How about we leave dessert until later? I can think of something even sweeter than those chocolates.'

Anna sighed as she wound her arms around his neck. She could get very used to them enjoying meals together like this. When Sam set her on her feet and reached for her hand, she didn't hesitate. She wanted to make love with him again as much as he did. She followed him to the stairs then groaned when the phone suddenly rang.

'I'll have to answer that in case it's work,' she explained ruefully.

'Of course.'

He leant against the newel post and watched while she picked up the receiver. Anna shivered when she felt his gaze travelling over her. It was incredibly erotic to know that he was imagining what would happen when they got up to the bedroom.

'Anna Carter,' she said crisply, before she got too carried away by the thought. As she'd suspected, it was the hospital and she listened with mounting concern as Wendy explained that Helen Denning was haemorrhaging badly.

'I'll be straight there, Wendy… No, there's no need to contact the duty surgeon. I'll attend to her myself.'

'Problems?' Sam said as she replaced the receiver in its rest.

'Yes. One of my patients who suffered a minor abruption. I was hoping to keep the pregnancy going but it's not to be.' She took her coat out of the cupboard under the stairs then suddenly remembered that she had left her car in town. 'Damn! How am I going to get there?'

'I'll run you in,' Sam offered immediately. 'I only had a sip of wine with lunch so there's no problem about me driving.'

'Thank heavens I did, too,' Anna said as she opened the front door. She checked that she had her keys then followed him down the path, smiling her thanks when he opened the car door for her. He'd always had impeccable manners and she appreciated the small courtesies he had always shown her.

It didn't take them long to reach the hospital. Sam drew up outside the maternity entrance and turned to her. 'I hope everything works out for your patient, Anna.'

'So do I.' She reached for the doorhandle then paused. 'Thank you for everything, Sam. I wasn't looking forward to this Christmas but you made it very special for me.'

'Ditto,' he murmured, leaning forward so he could kiss her lightly on the lips.

Anna sighed as she got out of the car and let herself into the unit. She could have stayed there all day and let him kiss her but duty called. Still, there would be time enough for them later. A feeling of happiness bubbled up inside her at the thought. They had a whole lifetime to look forward to now, not just a few snatched hours.

Sam drove back to the B&B after he dropped Anna off. His landlady had given him a key so he was able to let himself in without needing to talk to anyone. He didn't want anything to dilute this feeling of happiness that filled him, quite frankly.

He went straight up to his room and grabbed a change of clothes then headed for the bathroom. Officially, he wasn't due back at work until six that night but he had no intention of spending the rest of the day on his own. He would go back to the hospital and wait for Anna. She would need a lift home and if there was time, they might be able to snatch another few minutes together.

His body gave its own, very emphatic opinion about that plan of action and he chuckled. No change there, then. Whenever he had thought about Anna in the past, inevitably he had become aroused, and it was exactly the same now. What he needed was a cold shower to take the edge off his ardour until he could deal with it in a more satisfactory manner.

Ten minutes later, cold but clean, he was ready to leave. He had to drive through the town centre and he sighed as he drove past the ruins of the nightclub. There was a crew still working there, shoring up what remained of the building, but from what Sam could see the place would need to be demolished. Still, at least nobody had been killed and that had to be a miracle in itself.

He parked in front of the maternity unit then headed to the main entrance. Recalling the fuss that had been made the last time he had attempted to gain access to Maternity, he had decided that he would leave a message for Anna to let her know that he was there. He phoned the department and asked the sister to tell her to page him when she was finished and left it at that. After all, there was very little else he could have said. He could hardly have asked the woman to tell Anna how much he loved her.

He smiled to himself as he headed for the assessment ward to check on a couple of patients he had seen the previous night. The hospital gossips would have had a field day if that had got out!

'OK, so what's going on between you and that dishy Dr Kearney?'

Anna was on her way back from Theatre after delivering Helen Denning's baby when Wendy waylaid her. Helen had needed a hysterectomy once the baby boy had been delivered. She had lost a lot of blood and was very weak but Anna was confident that Helen would make a full recovery eventually. She was on her way to tell Brian Denning that but she stopped she heard what Wendy had said.

'What do you mean?'

'Only that the gorgeous Dr Kearney phoned while you were in Theatre and left a message to say that you should page him when you're through.' She handed Anna a slip of paper with the pager number written on it. 'It seems pretty clear to me but I'd still be interested to hear your take on it.'

Anna flushed when she saw the amusement on her friend's face. 'Sam very kindly drove me into work, that's all. I had to leave my car in town last night so I had no transport.'

'Oh, I see.' Wendy folded her arms. 'And how did he know that you needed to get here in a hurry?'

'I…um…' Anna realised her mistake too late. She bit her lip when Wendy chuckled.

'Aha! So I was right, then. You and Dr Dishy are an item. Come on, confess all. How long has it been going on?'

'It's not what you think, Wendy,' Anna said quietly. 'Sam and I knew each other before.'

'You did?' Wendy couldn't hide her surprise and Anna sighed. She might not want to talk about her relationship with Sam just yet, but neither did she want to lie to Wendy about it.

'Yes. We were married for five years, if you really want to know.'

'Oh, boy!' Wendy stared at her in amazement. 'You kept that quiet.'

'Yes. I didn't want people gossiping about us.'

'Well, they won't hear about it from me,' Wendy said firmly.

'Thanks. Sam and I...well, we need to be sure about what we want before we go public.'

'My lips are sealed.' Wendy made a little zipping action and Anna smiled.

'Thank you. Now, I'd better go and have a word with Brian Denning before the poor guy ends up in the coronary care unit.'

'OK. But if you need someone to talk to, Anna, I'm a good listener.'

'I'll remember that.'

Anna smiled at her friend then made her way to the relatives' room where she found Brian Denning pacing the floor. He spun round, his face turning ashen when he saw her.

'How is she?'

'Fine.' Anna steered him towards a chair. She'd seen far too many new fathers keel over to take any chances. 'Helen has lost a lot of blood and she's very weak, but I'm confident that she will make a full recovery in time. Unfortunately, I had to perform a hysterectomy because the uterus was so badly damaged and that will delay her recovery a little more.'

'Thank heavens!'

Brian put his head in his hands. Anna could see his

shoulders shaking and patted him on the back. 'Helen's going to be fine. She has the best incentive in the world to get better.'

'I know. It's just the thought that I could have lost her…' He gulped. 'How's the baby doing? It is a boy, like you told us it would be?'

Anna smiled. 'Yes, and he is absolutely fine. He weighed in at a very acceptable four pounds two ounces. He's in the premature baby unit at the moment, but that's purely routine for an infant who hasn't gone to term. His lungs are fine and he's breathing unaided, which is a very good sign.'

'That's really brilliant, Dr Carter.' Tears welled to the man's eyes and he laughed in embarrassment. 'You'll think I'm a right idiot for getting all emotional like this.'

'Not at all. I'd feel exactly the same,' Anna assured him, thinking how true that statement was. Pain lanced through her and she stood up abruptly, not wanting to think about her own situation at the moment. 'I'll take you through to the baby care unit so you can see your son. After that you'll be able to go and sit with Helen. She'll still be a bit groggy from the anaesthetic, but I'm sure she'll feel better once she knows you're there.'

She escorted Brian to the nursery and handed him over to the sister in charge then went to get changed. The unit was quiet so she decided that she wouldn't stay. Pritti was more than capable of handling things and she could always phone her at home if she needed any help.

Anna combed her hair then added a touch of lipstick

to her mouth, feeling her heart beating a shade faster than normal as she went into the office and picked up the phone. She gave the operator Sam's pager number then waited for him to call her back, which he did almost immediately. He'd obviously been waiting for her call and her heart raced even faster because it proved that he was as keen to be with her as she was to be with him.

Ten minutes later they were on their way back to her house. Although Sam would have to return to work later, at least they had a couple more hours to spend together. Anna glanced at him and felt a wave of love rise up inside her. The thought of spending another few hours with Sam was wonderful enough, but the thought of spending the rest of her life with him was so much better. At that moment there wasn't a single doubt in her mind about what she wanted from the future. She wanted to be with Sam for ever.

CHAPTER THIRTEEN

NEW Year came and went, and Sam felt as though he was starring in his very own dream. He and Anna spent every free minute together. Although, officially, he was still living at the B&B, he spent very little time there. When he wasn't at work he was at Anna's house, and he was loving every second of it, too.

Being back with her was such a joy. Not only did he get to sleep in the same bed as her—although not necessarily at the same time, thanks to the hours he worked—he kept rediscovering all sorts of things he had forgotten. He took great delight in watching her as she bustled about the house. The way she frowned in concentration as she tried out a new recipe for dinner made his heart overflow with tenderness; the way she folded up the dirty linen before putting it in the hamper made him want to hug her. Everything she did just made him love her more so that somedays he thought he would burst from the enormity of his feelings. And the best thing of all was knowing that she felt the same way about him.

There was another month of his contract to run when

he was summoned to the hospital manager's office and asked if he would consider taking the post on a permanent basis. Apparently, the registrar he was covering for had decided to leave and the powers that be were eager to obtain Sam's services.

It wasn't the first time that Sam had been asked to stay on. He was extremely good at his job and got on well with the people he worked with. However, it was the first time that he had seriously considered the idea. Staying in Dalverston was very appealing when it meant he could be with Anna.

He agreed to give the manager his decision by the end of the month and went back to work, mulling it over. Although they hadn't made any definite plans for the future, he was confident that Anna saw him as a permanent part of her life now. All they really needed to do was to regularise their relationship by getting married, but would she agree to marry him again, or would it be a step too far?

He knew how sensitive she still was about the issue of children and wasn't convinced that he had managed to persuade her he could be happy without them. He was terrified of bringing up the idea of them getting married in case it reawakened all her old fears. Marriage and family went hand in hand in many people's eyes, and Anna was no exception. He realised that it might be safer if he left things the way they were rather than risk upsetting her.

The weeks following that wonderful Christmas Day were the happiest Anna could remember. She woke each morning filled with anticipation and it was all down to Sam. Being with him again had shown her how much she had missed him. It was all the little things he did that made such a difference: the way he brought her a cup of coffee every morning and kissed her awake; the way he never, ever, forgot to tell her how beautiful she looked; the way he would just look at her and smile, and she would know immediately how much he loved her.

She was happier than she'd ever been. The only thing that could have made her life even better was if Sam had asked her to marry him again, but maybe that was too much to hope for. Maybe Sam was afraid to make that final commitment because they could never have children. Despite her new-found happiness, Anna couldn't quite shrug off the old fears.

It was mid-February when Anna was summoned to ED to see a patient. Sam wasn't on duty that day—he was working nights and Anna had seen him only briefly in passing that morning. As she asked for the duty doctor, she couldn't help wishing that he had been there so she could have spent a few extra minutes with him. She sighed as she followed the young registrar to Resus. She was acting like a lovesick teenager and she was way past the stage of being that!

The patient, a young woman in her twenties called Karen Simmons, had fallen downstairs. She was eighteen weeks pregnant and when Anna examined her, she could tell immediately that there were problems with the baby. She couldn't detect a heartbeat and a few gently probing questions soon elicited the information that the baby wasn't moving.

'I'm going to have you transferred to Maternity,' Anna explained, not wanting to voice her fears before it was absolutely necessary. 'I'd like to do a scan to see what's going on.'

'Why can't I feel my baby moving?' Karen pleaded.

'That's what we need to establish.'

Anna patted her hand then asked the registrar to call for a porter. This was a part of her job she hated. To see someone's hopes and dreams shattered this way was very hard, especially when it reminded her of the disappointments she and Sam had suffered.

As soon as Karen arrived at the maternity unit, Anna took her through to do the scan but, as she'd suspected, the baby had died. All that was left now was to deliver it and that was a deeply traumatic experience for everyone concerned. As she laid the tiny child in its mother's arms, Anna couldn't stop the tears trickling down her own face. It seemed so cruel that a precious life had been ended before it had begun.

Karen's partner arrived as Anna was leaving the side room where the young woman had been taken so she gently explained what had happened before she showed him in. Closing the door, she left the couple to try and come to terms with their loss. She had an antenatal clinic that afternoon and it was the best antidote she knew of after such a sad event.

Seeing the healthy mums helped a lot. Anna worked her way through her list, pleased to discover that most of her patients were doing well. There was just one mum she was concerned about as she was exhibiting early signs of pre-eclampsia so Anna arranged for her to be admitted while they monitored the situation. However, she was confident they had spotted the problem in time. By the time the last patient had been seen she felt much better and was looking forward to spending the evening at home with Sam.

She left the hospital, smiling when she spotted Sam's car parked outside the maternity unit. He often came to meet her from work just for the pleasure of driving her home. He wasn't in the vehicle, though, and she frowned as she wondered where he had got to. She finally spotted him talking to another man whom she immediately recognised as Karen's partner. Putting two and two together, she guessed that Sam had noticed that the poor man was upset and had gone to speak to him. It was so typical of him.

Her heart swelled with love as she walked over to them. Sam was the most caring person she had ever met. No wonder she loved him so much and wanted to spend the rest of her life with him.

She slowed down as she approached the bench, not wanting to intrude on the conversation. Sam was speaking now and she shivered when she heard the emotion in his voice. The other man's plight had obviously moved him, but that was to be expected. Losing a child was a highly emotive experience, and talking about it must have affected Sam deeply. In a funny way it felt as though she was eavesdropping and she half turned away then stopped when she heard what Sam said next.

'And, believe me, there is nothing I would love more than to have a family of my own, but if it's not to be then I just have to accept it.'

Anna felt a searing pain in her chest. All of a sudden it felt as though she couldn't breathe and she gasped. Sam had told her that it didn't matter if they could never have a child, but that certainly wasn't the impression she'd got from what she'd overheard. There had been resignation in his voice when he'd told the other man that he had accepted he would never have a family, and it simply reinforced every single one of her fears.

Sam was settling for second best. He was willing to put up with not having children because he loved her, but that wasn't good enough. She didn't want him making sacrifices for her, couldn't bear the thought that one day he would wish they hadn't got back together. She loved him too much for that, loved him far too much to allow him to settle for half-measures when he could have the lot: a woman to love and the family he longed for. No matter how much she loved him—and she did!—she couldn't let him waste his life by spending it with her.

Sam was waiting for Anna to finish work when he noticed a man come stumbling out of the maternity unit. The poor guy was obviously upset and Sam realised that he couldn't in all conscience leave him on his own in that state. He got out of the car and went over to him.

'Are you OK?' he asked, putting a friendly hand on the other man's shoulder.

'I don't know.' The man stared helplessly back at him. 'How could this have happened?'

He started weeping then, huge sobs racking his

entire body. Sam glanced round then steered him towards a nearby bench. 'Come along. It might help if you get it all off your chest.'

They sat down, although it was several minutes before the man was able to speak. Sam's heart went out to him when he heard about the baby dying. 'That's really tough on you both. Losing a child like that must be heartbreaking.'

'I just don't know what to do. Karen is beside herself and I don't know what to say to her to make it any better.'

'I don't think there's anything you can say,' Sam advised him. 'All you can do is be there for her. She's going to need a lot of support if she's to get through this.'

'I suppose you're right.' The man looked embarrassed as he wiped his eyes with his hand. 'Sorry. You must think I'm a right idiot for carrying on like this.'

'Of course I don't. I'd feel exactly the same if I were in your shoes,' Sam said truthfully. Although he and Anna had never got so far as actually conceiving a child, their hopes had been dashed so many times that he had a good idea how devastated the other man must feel.

'Thanks. Do you have any kids?'

Sam shook his head. 'I'm afraid not.'

The man dredged up a smile. 'You prefer the bachelor life, do you?'

'Not really. It just never worked out, that's all.' He sighed when he saw the question on the other man's face. 'My wife and I weren't able to have children, you see.'

'Oh, right. Sorry.' The man looked uncomfortable and Sam hurried to reassure him.

'It's OK. I've come to terms with it now.'

'Have you? I don't know if I ever would. I mean, having kids is just something you expect to happen, isn't it? You sort of take it for granted that you'll be a dad one day.'

'You do,' Sam admitted honestly. 'And believe me there is nothing I would love more than to have a family of my own, but if it's not to be then I just have to accept it.'

'You're a better man than I am if you can do that,' the man said bluntly. He stood up and held out his hand. 'Anyway, thanks for that, mate. I really appreciate it.'

'You're welcome.' Sam shook his hand then turned to go back to the car. It was only then that he spotted Anna and his heart turned over when he saw how pale and drawn she looked.

'I didn't see you there!' he exclaimed, hurrying over to her. He bent to kiss her then stopped when she turned her face away. 'What's wrong? Has something happened?'

'I heard what you said just now,' she said in a taut little voice.

'I'm not sure I understand what you mean,' he said slowly, his mind racing back over the conversation he'd had with the other man.

'You said that you would love to have a family,' she said sharply as she started walking across the car park.

Sam's heart sank as he hurried after her. He could have bitten off his tongue for making such an insensitive remark. 'I would never have said it if I'd known you were listening,' he apologised, catching hold of her arm and forcing her to stop.

'I know you wouldn't.' She stared back at him and he could see the hurt in her eyes. 'You would have skated round the truth to spare my feelings, but I don't want them spared, Sam. I don't want you to sacrifice your dreams for me.'

'I'm not!' He gripped hold of her arm, terrified that she would rush off before he had the chance to sort this out. 'Being back with you again is everything I've ever dreamed of, Anna. You know that.'

'Do I?' She gave a bitter little laugh. 'You told me that you didn't *care* if we couldn't have children, but that wasn't what you told that man just now. You'll have to excuse me if I'm a little confused as to which version is true.'

'Both.' He gave her a little shake, unbearably hurt by the fact that she still doubted how he felt about her. Hadn't he shown her these past few weeks just how much he loved her? Pain bubbled up inside him but he had to rein in his feelings if he hoped to convince her that he wanted to be with her no matter what.

'I love you, Anna, and I want nothing more than to spend the rest of my life with you.'

'And what about the family you long for?' she taunted. 'Where does that feature in your plans?'

'It doesn't. All right, so I'll admit it—if we could have kids, that would be fantastic. I'd be the happiest man alive and I won't deny it. But we can't have children and I have accepted that, as I've told you before.'

'What you really mean is that you've settled for second best, and I'm afraid that isn't good enough for me, Sam.'

She shrugged off his hand and stepped back, her face set, her whole body rigid. Sam half reached towards her then let his hands fall to his sides when he realised how pointless it was to try and get through to her at that moment. Anna was shutting him out again and nothing he said or did would break through her defences.

'You have never been second best, Anna, and you never will be. I love you with all my heart and I want to be with you and only you, but you have to believe that yourself for it to mean anything.'

She didn't say anything, didn't give any sign at all that she'd heard him even, and Sam felt his heart start to shatter into dozens of tiny pieces. It was exactly what had happened before. Anna had shut him out then, closed her mind and her heart to the truth because she hadn't wanted to hear it. Could he really go through that kind of anguish again? Could he gather up the pieces of his heart and weld them back together if she decided that she no longer wanted to be with him this time, too?

The thought was more than he could bear. He swung round and strode back to his car. His hands were shaking as he slid the key into the ignition and it took him a couple of goes before he managed to start the engine. It felt as though he had suffered an almighty blow but he should be used to the feeling because it wasn't the first time it had happened but the second.

Anna had shut him out of her life three years ago and

she was doing exactly the same thing again now. The only difference was that this time he wasn't going to try and change her mind. There was only so much pain a person could suffer in one lifetime and he had surpassed his limit. This time he was going to do what she wanted and disappear from her life for good.

CHAPTER FOURTEEN

THE days passed in a blur. Anna went to work each morning although she couldn't recall a thing she had done when she got home at night. She'd heard on the hospital grapevine that Sam was leaving, although he hadn't told her so himself.

They hadn't spoken since what had happened in the car park. He had stopped meeting her after work and no longer came round to her house, and she missed him dreadfully. But even though she longed to see him and try to sort everything out, she refused to do so. Sam would be better off without her and one day he would realise that himself.

February brought some of the worst weather Dalverston had ever seen. Heavy snow made travelling a nightmare. What made it worse was that Anna was feeling really worn out all the time. She put it down to the fact that she had to leave home earlier than usual to allow for the icy road conditions, but she didn't feel any better once the weather improved. She felt nauseous all the time and weepy, too, although that was to be expected after what had happened between her and Sam.

She was in the middle of a busy antenatal clinic one afternoon when it suddenly dawned on her that there might be another reason for the way she was feeling: she'd not had a period since December. Although her cycle had always been irregular, she'd never been so late before, and it immediately triggered alarm bells. Was it possible that she was pregnant?

She was a bundle of nerves as she saw her patient out then told the nurse she needed to fetch some papers from her office. There was a dispensary in the hospital foyer so she headed straight there, bought a pregnancy testing kit and took it to the ladies' lavatories.

She and Sam hadn't bothered using any contraception. With their track record there'd been no point, plus she knew from what he had told her that he hadn't slept with anyone else during their time apart. The thought that their love-making could have resulted in the one thing they had dreamed of having was almost too much to take in, but after she did the test, the proof was clear to see. She was pregnant. She was having Sam's baby!

After leaving Dalverston, Sam took a couple of short-term contracts while he worked out what he intended to do with his life. He knew that he'd been drifting along since the divorce but now it was time he made some plans for the future. The fact that Anna hadn't made any attempt to see him before he had left simply proved that he had to forget about her. It wasn't going to be an easy thing to do because he loved her so much and longed to be with her, but he couldn't keep on torturing himself. He had to forget about the past and start living again.

In the end, he decided to return to Australia. With his skills, he had no problem getting the necessary work permit and soon found himself a job at a hospital in Sydney. His flight was booked for the end of the month and as he had so few possessions, making the move would be pretty straightforward. It was the emotional baggage that would weigh him down, the thought of what might have been, but he would get over that in time. All he had to do was forget about Anna—if he ever could.

He left work one night, worn out after a double shift. The hospital where he was working was in the centre of Manchester and it was extremely busy there. As he headed out of the building, he couldn't help wishing that he could just get on the plane and leave. The sooner he got away from England and all the unhappy memories it held for him, the better.

'Sam.'

Sam stopped dead when he heard someone say his name. As though it was happening in slow motion, he turned and felt his heart leap when he saw Anna standing behind him. She was wearing a heavy winter coat and boots, and her hair was tousled by the wind, but she looked so beautiful that he felt tears immediately start to his eyes.

'If I'm dreaming, please don't wake me up,' he muttered.

'It isn't a dream.' She took a step towards him. 'I contacted the agency and they told me where you were working. I…I need to talk to you, Sam.'

Sam's head was reeling. He knew that whatever

Anna had to say to him must be important otherwise she wouldn't have gone to the trouble of tracking him down, but the thought was just too much to deal with when he was so tired and stressed. He stared dumbly back at her and Anna obviously mistook his silence as an indication that he didn't want to talk to her.

She took a step back. 'I'm sorry. Obviously, I shouldn't have come. I apologise for bothering you.'

She turned and hurried across the car park. Sam remained rooted to the spot for a moment before he realised what was happening. If he didn't pull himself together Anna would leave, and that would be the last he ever saw of her!

Fear added wings to his feet as he raced after her. 'Anna, wait!'

She must have heard him shouting but, if anything, she speeded up. Sam gritted his teeth as he summoned up the last ounce of strength he had left in his weary body and managed to catch up with her as she was about to unlock her car. Doubling over at the waist, he sucked in several lungfuls of much-needed air before he managed to speak.

'You…can't…leave…like…this,' he panted. 'You've… got…to…tell…me…why…you…came…here.'

'It was a mistake.' She jiggled the keys in her hand and her eyes were haunted as she stared at him. 'It's obvious that you don't want anything more to do with me, Sam, and I don't blame you after what happened. Just forget about it.'

She slid behind the wheel but Sam wasn't about to give up after the effort he'd put in. Leaning into the car, he deftly removed the keys from her hand. 'You're not going anywhere until you tell me why you went to all the trouble of tracking me down.'

'I told you to forget about it,' she said shortly, staring through the windscreen.

'Just tell me, Anna.' He crouched down beside the car and turned her to face him. 'Whatever's happened, we can sort it out. I promise you that, my darling.'

'Do you really believe that?' she whispered, her voice catching.

'Yes.' Sam took another deep breath but there wasn't enough oxygen in the universe to fill his aching lungs at that moment. His voice was hoarse when he continued, but it was rich with emotion and that more than made up for everything else. 'I love you with every fibre of my being, Anna. There's no problem too big that we can't solve if we do it together.'

'I love you, too.' Tears started to trickle down her cheeks. Leaning forward, she pressed her mouth to his and Sam felt as though the world was about explode with joy. There were rockets going off in his head, stars bursting, whole planets whizzing about the sky because Anna—his beautiful, wonderful, Anna—had kissed him.

He felt drunk with happiness when she drew back, so elated that it was difficult to form a rational thought. But one did surface, proving that at least a bit of his mind had managed to retain some sanity. 'We can't talk here, Anna. Where are you staying?'

'At the hotel near the television studio.'

Sam nodded. 'I know the place. You head back there

and I'll follow you.' He closed the door then paused and kissed her again, his eyes smiling into hers. 'That should keep me going for a few minutes but I will need a top-up fairly soon, I warn you.'

'I'm sure that can be arranged,' she said, smiling up at him.

Sam would have kissed her again only he knew that if he did so it would lead to something more, and a hospital car park wasn't the place for what he had in mind.

He hurried to his car and followed her back to her hotel. She had a ground-floor room so it was only a short distance from the car park, but it was far enough. Anna unlocked the door and the next minute they were in each others arms, kissing.

'Better close this before someone comes along,' he growled, kicking the door shut behind them.

He kissed her again, savouring the taste and feel of her lips, the softness of her body, the scent of her skin. He had dreamed about her every night since he'd left Dalverston and now he wouldn't have to be content with just his dreams because he had her here in his arms where she was meant to be. And this time he wouldn't let her go. This time he intended to keep her in his arms for ever more!

Anna could feel her heart racing with joy as Sam kissed her. She hadn't known what to expect when she'd set off that morning. She'd been very aware that he could have refused to speak to her, but he'd soon erased her fears. Sam loved her and when he found out what she wanted to tell him, he would be over the moon.

Happiness bubbled up inside her as she drew back and smiled at him. 'I think we should take off our coats, don't you?'

'Why stop at the coats?' he argued with a wolfish smile.

'We won't.' She kissed him softly on the mouth then stepped back before he could deepen the kiss. 'But there's something I need to tell you first, Sam. Something important.'

'Hmm, I'm not sure if I like the sound of that,' he said, only half-joking.

'Oh, yes, you will,' she assured him, slipping off her coat. She tossed it over a chair then sat down on the bed and patted the mattress beside her. 'Come and sit down.'

Sam shed his coat and took his seat. Capturing her hand, he pressed a kiss to her palm. Anna shivered when she felt his lips brush her skin. She longed to make love with him, too, but she wanted to tell him about the baby before anything else happened.

'There's something I need to tell you, Sam,' she said again, wondering how to break the news to him. He would be thrilled, of course, but it would still come as a shock and she wanted to broach the subject with care.

'So you keep saying,' he murmured, nuzzling her neck.

'I know.' Anna shivered appreciatively but she steeled herself against the sensations that were rushing through her. 'You'll have to forgive me for repeating myself, but I don't want to give you too much of a shock.'

'A shock?' He drew back and looked at her in concern. 'Has something happened?'

Anna blushed. 'Hmm, you could say that.'

'Then tell me what it is.'

Anna took a quick breath then launched into her tale. 'After you left Dalverston, I didn't feel really like myself,' she began.

'You're not ill, are you, Anna?' he interrupted her anxiously.

'No, not all,' she said hurriedly when she saw the fear on his face. 'I'm fine, Sam, really I am. In fact, I couldn't be better.'

'Then what is it?' He captured her hands and held them tightly as though he was willing her to find the courage to tell him her news.

Anna smiled at him, relishing this moment which she had waited such a long time for. 'I'm pregnant.'

'Pregnant?' he repeated, and she laughed.

'Yes! I'm having a baby, Sam. *Our* baby!'

Sam felt the room start to spin. He knew that if he hadn't been sitting down, he would have fallen over. He stared at Anna, unable to hide his shock. 'Are you sure?'

'Yes. I did a test and then another one to make certain. I even got Pritti to check, although she didn't know the sample came from me, of course.' She smiled at him, her beautiful face alight with happiness. 'We're having a baby, Sam, at long last.'

Sam didn't know what to say. After all the years they had spent longing for this moment to happen, it should have been easy to know what to do, but that had been then and this was now. And now it was far more complicated.

He stood up abruptly, unable to give voice to all the feelings that were churning around inside him. Oh, he was thrilled at the thought of being a father—who wouldn't be? However, there was a sinking feeling inside him he couldn't ignore.

Anna hadn't come after him because she had missed him so much that she couldn't carry on without him. She had come to tell him about the baby. Maybe it was wrong to feel this way, but he couldn't help feeling hurt that he hadn't been enough for her on his own—she'd needed his child as well.

'Sam? What is it? Aren't you pleased?'

He heard the uncertainty in her voice and cursed himself for being so selfish. Anna had waited such a long time for this to happen and been through so much—he certainly didn't want to ruin it for her.

'Of course I'm pleased. I'm thrilled!' He went and knelt in front of her. 'It's just so hard to take it all in.'

'I know.' She gave a bubbly little laugh and that made him feel even worse. He should be celebrating with her instead of being plagued by all these stupid doubts.

'I never thought it would happen. I'd given up all hope of having a baby so it's just like a miracle to suddenly find myself pregnant.'

'It is,' he agreed, forcing himself to smile at her.

'Are you sure, Sam?' She took his face between her hands and looked deep into his eyes. 'You are happy about the baby, aren't you?'

'Yes. I just wish…' He broke off, not wanting to spoil things by admitting his fears.

'What? I can tell that something is wrong, Sam, so please tell me what it is.'

'I just wish that I'd been enough for you, and that you hadn't needed a baby to want me as well,' he admitted roughly.

'Is that what you think? That I wouldn't want you if I wasn't pregnant?'

'Yes.' He shrugged. 'I understand how you feel, Anna, really I do. You've longed for this to happen and now that it is has, you must be over the moon.'

'I am. It's a dream come true, although I thought it would be the same for both of us.'

'It is!' he assured her when he saw the sadness in her eyes. He kissed her lightly on the mouth then smiled at her. 'I'm thrilled, Anna. It's a miracle as you said, our very own Christmas miracle.'

'But you still have reservations,' she said in a tight little voice.

'Not about the baby. How could I when it's something we've both longed for?'

He kissed her again, wanting to reassure her that he was as delighted as she was about this unexpected turn of events. It seemed to work because she kissed him back and he sighed in relief when he felt her melt into his arms. He didn't want anything to spoil their reunion, and definitely not these stupid doubts he had.

They made love and it was an act of intense joy for both of them. Knowing that Anna was carrying his child made it an incredibly moving experience. Sam was overwhelmed with tenderness as he stroked her breasts and the gentle curve of her stomach. There was little sign of her pregnancy yet, but to know that his child was lying beneath his hand touched him more deeply than anything had ever done.

As they drifted off to sleep a short time later, he knew that he had been given something so precious that he would never take it for granted. He would love and care for this child until the end of his days, just as he would love and care for its mother. And if his happiness was tinged by a faint sadness that Anna might never feel as deeply about him, he pushed the thought to the very back his mind. He wouldn't spoil what he had by wishing for more.

CHAPTER FIFTEEN

ONCE her initial tiredness and nausea disappeared, Anna positively bloomed. She loved being pregnant and enjoyed every moment of the experience. Everyone apart from Wendy had been stunned at first when she had announced that she was having a baby and explained that Sam was the father, but they had soon accepted it. The fact that Sam had returned to Dalverston and taken up the senior registrar's post in ED had helped, too. Everyone knew they were a couple now and accepted them as such. The only blot on the horizon, in fact, was how she could convince Sam that he'd been wrong about her only wanting him because of the baby. However, there never seemed to be a good moment to raise the subject so she let it ride. Sam would realise very soon that his fear was groundless.

Anna was nearing her eighth month and thinking about her forthcoming maternity leave when she woke up one morning and knew immediately that something was wrong. Climbing out of bed, she went into the bathroom and felt her heart turn over when she discovered to her dismay that she was bleeding. She'd had several scans done, including one of the new 4D scans which had showed every detail of the baby in her womb. She had been confident that everything had been progressing as it should do so it was a double shock. Sam was working nights that week and he wasn't back from work so she phoned the ED and left a message for him to say that she was calling for an ambulance. When she arrived at the maternity unit, he was waiting for her, along with Pritti and Janet Clarke the senior midwife.

Anna felt tears start to pour down her face when she saw Sam. She had managed to contain her fear up till then but she couldn't hold it back any longer. 'I've started bleeding,' she told him, gulping back sobs. 'I don't know why. Maybe it's because I've worked too long…'

'Shh.' He bent and kissed her. 'It's not your fault, Anna, my darling, so stop beating yourself up. Nobody could have taken better care of their baby than you've done.'

'But what if I lose our baby? I couldn't bear it, Sam, not after everything we've been through.'

'You are not going to lose our baby,' he said firmly. 'Even if it has to be delivered immediately, you know better than me that he has an excellent chance of surviving.'

'But terrible things still happen,' Anna wept, overwhelmed by fear. They had reached the delivery suite and she nodded when Pritti told her that they needed to move her onto a bed.

As soon as that was accomplished, the team set to work. Anna knew the routine so well but it was very different being a patient. Her heart was thumping as Janet set up the foetal monitor. When she heard the sound of her baby's heartbeat echoing around the room, she was overwhelmed with relief.

'Good strong heartbeat,' Janet announced.

'That's excellent,' Pritti said, coming over to the bed. 'Now, let's take a look at you, Anna, and see if we can work out what's happening.'

Anna lay quite still while her registrar carried out an extremely thorough examination. Pritti decided to do a scan as well to see if she could pinpoint the cause of the bleeding. Anna could feel her stomach churning as she waited for the machine to be set up. She didn't know how she was going to cope if anything happened to this precious child.

'It's going to be fine, Anna.' Sam bent and kissed her.

'But there's so many things that can go wrong,' Anna said despairingly. 'I couldn't bear it if we lost the baby, Sam. Really I couldn't.'

'We're not going to lose him,' he repeated.

He kissed her again then moved aside so Pritti could do the scan. She had turned the monitor screen away from them and Anna tried to curb her impatience. She had to trust Pritti to do her job and not interfere.

'I can see what the problem is now.' Pritti turned the monitor towards them. 'The placenta has separated from the wall of the uterus just here.'

Anna's heart sank as she studied the screen. 'It's quite a large separation, isn't it?'

'It is.' Pritti looked at her and Sam. 'I doubt we will be able to keep the pregnancy going, Anna. In my opinion, it will be safer for you and the baby if we deliver him now.'

'But he's only thirty-two weeks,' Anna protested, knowing the registrar was right. The danger to the baby if nothing was done was immense. The placenta supplied oxygen and nutrients to the child as well as removing waste products from its system. If it became fully detached, her baby would be in grave danger.

'Yes, I know that. But we've delivered lots of babies who are far more premature and they've survived,' Pritti pointed out gently.

Anna closed her eyes. It was like a nightmare. Having this happen was something she had never anticipated. 'We don't have a choice, do we?' she said brokenly.

Pritti went to phone Theatre, leaving her and Sam alone. Anna clung to his hand, unable to put her fears into words, but he knew what she was thinking anyway.

'Our little one will be fine, sweetheart,' he said softly, stroking her hair. 'He's a good size and thirty-two weeks isn't that early, is it?'

'I'm just so scared,' she whispered.

'I am too, but everything will be fine, you'll see.' He kissed her on the mouth, his eyes filled with such love that Anna felt all her emotions well up and spill over.

'I love you so much, Sam. I know you think that I only want you because of this baby, but it isn't true. I've always wanted you but I was so afraid of ruining your life and that's why I asked you for a divorce. It's why I let you leave Dalverston after Christmas, too. I didn't want to lose you but I wanted you to have the chance of having the family you deserve.'

Tears welled into his eyes. 'I thought I wasn't enough for you,' he admitted brokenly.

'You've always been enough for me, Sam, and you always will be, no matter what happens today.'

There was no time to say anything else because Pritti was waiting to take her through to Theatre. Sam went with her and insisted on staying by her side while she was prepped. Having him there helped enormously. As Anna was wheeled into Theatre a short time later, she knew in her heart that everything would be all right. Their miracle wasn't going to end here. It was going to last a whole lifetime.

EPILOGUE

SAM checked his watch for the umpteenth time. He had a very important date and he didn't intend to be late for it. He grinned as he watched the minute hand complete its final circuit of the dial. This was it, then, the moment he'd been waiting for had arrived at last.

He left the ED and headed up to the maternity unit, making straight for the nursery when he got there. Anna was already there and she looked round and smiled when she heard him coming along the corridor.

'You look exactly how I feel.'

'I can't remember ever feeling this excited before,' he admitted, dropping a kiss on her lips.

He turned and looked through the nursery window, his face softening as he studied his son. Little Archie Samuel Kearney had been a model patient following his early arrival into the world. He had put on enough weight now for them to take him home that day, in fact.

'He's gorgeous, isn't he?' Anna said dreamily.

'He is. Just like his mum.' Sam took her into his arms. 'Have I told you lately how much I love you?' he said, buzzing her lips with a kiss.

'Not since last night,' she murmured, kissing him back.

Sam sighed when he felt her nestle against him. What Anna had told him prior to their son's birth had cleared his mind of any doubts about her feelings for him. She loved him and wanted him, and that made him feel like the luckiest man alive. There was just one small issue that needed clearing up now but he was confident that it wouldn't pose a problem.

'Hmm, that was very remiss of me.' He kissed her again then let her go. Feeling in his pocket he took out a velvet covered box. 'I love you, Anna, and I want to spend the rest of my life making you happy. Will you do me the honour of becoming my wife?'

Anna gasped when he opened the box and showed her the beautiful diamond and emerald ring. 'It's gorgeous, Sam!'

'So are you.' He slipped the ring on her finger then kissed her hand. 'Is that a yes, then?'

'Oh, most definitely!' She put her arms around him and hugged him then laughed when she realised that most of the staff in the nursery were watching what was going on and applauding.

Sam chuckled as he slid his arm around her waist. 'You can't go back on your decision now. There's too many witnesses.'

'I shall never go back on my decision,' she said firmly. She grasped his hand and led him to the door. 'Now, let's go and tell our son that his mummy and daddy are getting married.'

0907 Gen Std HB

MILLS & BOON
Pure reading pleasure

OCTOBER 2007 HARDBACK TITLES

ROMANCE

The Desert Sheikh's Captive Wife *Lynne Graham*	978 0 263 19700 6
His Christmas Bride *Helen Brooks*	978 0 263 19701 3
The Demetrios Bridal Bargain *Kim Lawrence*	978 0 263 19702 0
The Spanish Prince's Virgin Bride *Sandra Marton*	978 0 263 19703 7
Bought: One Island, One Bride *Susan Stephens*	978 0 263 19704 4
One Night in His Bed *Christina Hollis*	978 0 263 19705 1
The Greek Tycoon's Innocent Mistress *Kathryn Ross*	978 0 263 19706 8
The Italian's Chosen Wife *Kate Hewitt*	978 0 263 19707 5
The Millionaire Tycoon's English Rose *Lucy Gordon*	978 0 263 19708 2
Snowbound with Mr Right *Judy Christenberry*	978 0 263 19709 9
The Boss's Little Miracle *Barbara McMahon*	978 0 263 19710 5
His Christmas Angel *Michelle Douglas*	978 0 263 19711 2
Their Greek Island Reunion *Carol Grace*	978 0 263 19712 9
Win, Lose…or Wed! *Melissa McClone*	978 0 263 19713 6
Their Little Christmas Miracle *Jennifer Taylor*	978 0 263 19714 3
A Pregnant Nurse's Christmas Wish *Meredith Webber*	978 0 263 19715 0

HISTORICAL

Housemaid Heiress *Elizabeth Beacon*	978 0 263 19775 4
Marrying Captain Jack *Anne Herries*	978 0 263 19776 1
My Lord Footman *Claire Thornton*	978 0 263 19777 8

MEDICAL™

Christmas-Eve Baby *Caroline Anderson*	978 0 263 19820 1
Long-Lost Son: Brand New Family *Lilian Darcy*	978 0 263 19821 8
Twins for a Christmas Bride *Josie Metcalfe*	978 0 263 19822 5
The Doctor's Very Special Christmas *Kate Hardy*	978 0 263 19823 2

0907 Gen Std LP

Pure reading pleasure

OCTOBER 2007 LARGE PRINT TITLES

ROMANCE

The Ruthless Marriage Proposal *Miranda Lee* 978 0 263 19487 6
Bought for the Greek's Bed *Julia James*   978 0 263 19488 3
The Greek Tycoon's Virgin Mistress   978 0 263 19489 0
Chantelle Shaw
The Sicilian's Red-Hot Revenge *Kate Walker*   978 0 263 19490 6
A Mother for the Tycoon's Child   978 0 263 19491 3
Patricia Thayer
The Boss and His Secretary *Jessica Steele*   978 0 263 19492 0
Billionaire on her Doorstep *Ally Blake*   978 0 263 19493 7
Married by Morning *Shirley Jump*   978 0 263 19494 4

HISTORICAL

A Scoundrel of Consequence *Helen Dickson*   978 0 263 19406 7
An Innocent Courtesan *Elizabeth Beacon*   978 0 263 19407 4
The King's Champion *Catherine March*   978 0 263 19408 1

MEDICAL™

His Very Own Wife and Child   978 0 263 19367 1
Caroline Anderson
The Consultant's New-Found Family   978 0 263 19368 8
Kate Hardy
City Doctor, Country Bride *Abigail Gordon*   978 0 263 19369 5
The Emergency Doctor's Daughter *Lucy Clark* 978 0 263 19370 1
A Child to Care For *Dianne Drake*   978 0 263 19545 3
His Pregnant Nurse *Laura Iding*   978 0 263 19546 0

Pure reading pleasure

NOVEMBER 2007 HARDBACK TITLES

ROMANCE

The Italian Billionaire's Ruthless Revenge *Jacqueline Baird*	978 0 263 19716 7
Accidentally Pregnant, Conveniently Wed *Sharon Kendrick*	978 0 263 19717 4
The Sheikh's Chosen Queen *Jane Porter*	978 0 263 19718 1
The Frenchman's Marriage Demand *Chantelle Shaw*	978 0 263 19719 8
The Millionaire's Convenient Bride *Catherine George*	978 0 263 19720 4
Expecting His Love-Child *Carol Marinelli*	978 0 263 19721 1
The Greek Tycoon's Unexpected Wife *Annie West*	978 0 263 19722 8
The Italian's Captive Virgin *India Grey*	978 0 263 19723 5
Her Hand in Marriage *Jessica Steele*	978 0 263 19724 2
The Sheikh's Unsuitable Bride *Liz Fielding*	978 0 263 19725 9
The Bridesmaid's Best Man *Barbara Hannay*	978 0 263 19726 6
A Mother in a Million *Melissa James*	978 0 263 19727 3
The Rancher's Doorstep Baby *Patricia Thayer*	978 0 263 19728 0
Moonlight and Roses *Jackie Braun*	978 0 263 19729 7
Their Miracle Child *Gill Sanderson*	978 0 263 19730 3
Single Dad, Nurse Bride *Lynne Marshall*	978 0 263 19731 0

HISTORICAL

The Vanishing Viscountess *Diane Gaston*	978 0 263 19778 5
A Wicked Liaison *Christine Merrill*	978 0 263 19779 2
Virgin Slave, Barbarian King *Louise Allen*	978 0 263 19780 8

MEDICAL™

The Italian's New-Year Marriage Wish *Sarah Morgan*	978 0 263 19824 9
The Doctor's Longed-For Family *Joanna Neil*	978 0 263 19825 6
Their Special-Care Baby *Fiona McArthur*	978 0 263 19826 3
A Family for the Children's Doctor *Dianne Drake*	978 0 263 19827 0

1007 Gen Std LP

Pure reading pleasure

NOVEMBER 2007 LARGE PRINT TITLES

ROMANCE

Bought: The Greek's Bride *Lucy Monroe*	978 0 263 19495 1
The Spaniard's Blackmailed Bride *Trish Morey*	978 0 263 19496 8
Claiming His Pregnant Wife *Kim Lawrence*	978 0 263 19497 5
Contracted: A Wife for the Bedroom *Carol Marinelli*	978 0 263 19498 2
The Forbidden Brother *Barbara McMahon*	978 0 263 19499 9
The Lazaridis Marriage *Rebecca Winters*	978 0 263 19500 2
Bride of the Emerald Isle *Trish Wylie*	978 0 263 19501 9
Her Outback Knight *Melissa James*	978 0 263 19502 6

HISTORICAL

Dishonour and Desire *Juliet Landon*	978 0 263 19409 8
An Unladylike Offer *Christine Merrill*	978 0 263 19410 4
The Roman's Virgin Mistress *Michelle Styles*	978 0 263 19411 1

MEDICAL™

A Bride for Glenmore *Sarah Morgan*	978 0 263 19371 8
A Marriage Meant To Be *Josie Metcalfe*	978 0 263 19372 5
Dr Constantine's Bride *Jennifer Taylor*	978 0 263 19373 2
His Runaway Nurse *Meredith Webber*	978 0 263 19374 9
The Rescue Doctor's Baby Miracle *Dianne Drake*	978 0 263 19547 7
Emergency at Riverside Hospital *Joanna Neil*	978 0 263 19548 4